His Christmas Joy

Christmas Town Book 7

by

Ginny Baird

His Christmas Joy

Christmas Town Book 7

by

Ginny Baird

Published by

Winter Wedding Press

Print Edition

ISBN 978-1-942058-38-0

Edited by Sally Knapp
Cover Design by Dar Albert

Ginny Baird's

HIS CHRISTMAS JOY

Chapter One

JOY HUNCHED HER shoulders against the wind and trudged through the pelting snow, making her way up North Main Street toward the post office near the roundabout. She had a backpack slung over one shoulder, containing a huge haul of mail. Her dad, Walt, and his new wife, Gloria, were sending out a slew of Christmas cards this year. Their six-month-old son, Xavier, and sweet yellow Labrador, Gitana, were highlighted in the photo display, which also included separate shots of Joy, which she'd sent them from Italy, and her twin sister, Noelle, who was in graduate school in North Carolina. Gloria had hinted that maybe this year—with Joy being home—they could get a picture of the whole family together. Perhaps around one of the gorgeously decorated Christmas trees at their family residence, the Christmas Inn.

Joy was happy to be home. She simply couldn't help the sting of rejection she felt at Giacomo not coming with her. Joy had assumed they'd be spending the holidays in Christmas Town like they had last year. Joy had spent every Christmas of her life here, except for that college year when she'd been studying abroad in Italy. While she understood Giacomo's argument for starting a holiday rotation, this wasn't the best time to begin one. Joy had a new baby half-brother that she hadn't yet met, and she'd wanted to come home very badly to see him.

Giacomo, on the other hand, argued that he'd made the exception last year by visiting Joy's family at Christmastime. This year, it was their turn to see his folks. Giacomo's parents, who occupied a lavish home overlooking the Grand Canal in Venice, were currently snow skiing in the Italian Alps, where they had a "little winter cottage." The Romanos also owned a villa in Tuscany, and an additional vacation home on the Costa del Sol in the south of Spain.

As Joy hadn't yet met Giacomo's older sister, Margherita, who lived with her husband and kids in Paris, Giacomo had hoped Joy could make the skiing trip. Joy had wanted to go, she really had. And, she actually would have loved to meet Giacomo's gregarious older sister, who she'd heard so much about. But, Joy hadn't even had a chance to meet little Xavier! She'd missed his birth in June, as she'd already moved to Florence by then. Plus, it was the holidays, and Joy was feeling really homesick.

Giacomo and Joy, who'd been dating since Joy spent her junior year in Italy, had mutually agreed she would move there to be closer to Giacomo, while he finished his architectural studies. Joy had paired up with an American college friend of hers as roommates, and spent several days a week serving as a docent at Il Duomo. In her free time, Joy painted so many glorious city scenes. Her favorite was a perspective on Florence from the nearby town, Fiesole, which she got to by bus. She'd managed to transport the large oil canvas home, and planned to give it to her dad and stepmom as a Christmas gift. If they liked it enough, she was hopeful they would hang it somewhere at the Christmas Inn.

Joy passed her grandparents' cool Victorian home on the left as she neared the Grand Hotel. A collection of three townhomes, collectively called Sisters' Row, was across the street from her. The Snow Globe Gallery, which nestled next to Sisters' Row, was also on the corner with Santa Claus Lane. The Merry Market sat on the corner across from the gallery, also framing the T-intersection that faced the ornate façade of the Grand Hotel. The former hotel was four stories tall on top of a basement, with formidable steps leading up to its fancy front door.

Since its restoration a few years ago, the Grand Hotel now housed several working artists' studios, along with a restaurant and a huge ballroom on the first floor, and a children's theater on the fourth floor upstairs. At the moment, a guy in a field coat and faded jeans was hustling down the building's front steps, his chin ducked low to avoid the onslaught of snow. The youngish-looking man with chiseled cheekbones wore his dark hair tucked under a wool cap but no gloves, and heavy snow boots. He reached the sidewalk at the same time Joy arrived at the front of the Grand Hotel, and looked up.

Soulful gray eyes met Joy's and her heart skipped a beat.

Devon Slade was the hottie that Joy had dated in high school, and during her first two years of college. They'd amicably parted ways when she went off to Italy for her junior year abroad, and Devon had stayed home to focus on his art, which was woodworking. Things had gone really well for Devon, too. He now had his own studio in the Grand Hotel on the third floor.

Though Joy had previously run into her old high school boyfriend on numerous occasions in Christmas Town, that fact didn't stop her heart from pounding harder each time she saw him. Not that Joy was interested in Devon any longer. What they'd had between them was history, and they were both totally over it.

Devon's face lit up with surprise when he saw her. "Joy? I didn't know you were coming home?"

"I...er...yeah!"

"Noelle said you were going skiing, or something, in the Italian Alps?"

That was the other thing that bothered Joy. Her twin sister, Noelle, had become best buds with Devon. Not that they were dating or anything. And, Noelle had actually been careful to clear their friendship with Joy first. But, what could Joy say? No, you can't go to the Christmas Town Ball with my ex—not once, but two years in a row? It was fine with Joy. Totally fine. She'd been away in Italy that first year, anyway. And last year, Giacomo had been in Christmas Town to take Joy to the ball. Which had been an amazingly awesome time. Because she loved Giacomo a lot. He was her destiny. Not...Devon Slade.

Devon eyed Joy curiously as she continued. "I *was* going skiing, but then changed my mind. Wanted to come home. You know..." She shrugged, the backpack on her right shoulder growing heavy. "Meet Xavier."

Devon smiled fondly. "Cute kid."

That was the other thing. Devon had apparently come for Thanksgiving dinner at the Christmas Inn! Thanksgiving, of all things! A "family" dinner. Joy's cute new uncle, David Chavez, had been there with his sweet girlfriend, Liz. Noelle had been home from school...and Joy had been stuck in Florence. Which was okay, since nobody celebrated the American holiday there anyway. She'd barely even thought about it.

"You headed my way?" Devon asked, pointing south.

"To the post office, yeah!"

"I'm stepping out to Jolly Bean Java," he informed her. "Got to get my mid-morning fix." His smile gleamed and Joy wished that Devon would stop that. Looking so much better than she recalled...during those few, extremely rare times that she thought about him. Which was only occasionally, though Joy assumed that was natural. Everybody reminisced about former flames once in a while. No big deal.

Joy gave a light-hearted laugh, as they both resumed walking, passing Devon's parents' business, South Pole Pottery, on their left. "I know what you mean! I like my coffee, too."

"Bet it's pretty good in Italy."

"It is!"

"So...?" Devon paused in front of All Things Christmas, which was directly across the street from the coffee shop. "Giacomo come with you?"

"Nuh-uh." Joy smiled tightly, not willing to inform her former boyfriend that she and her current boyfriend had recently had an epic fight. "Not this time!"

"Well, that's too bad. I hope everything's all right?" Devon studied her curiously and Joy guessed he was trying to read her. "With Giacomo, I mean."

"Oh yeah!" Joy lied through her teeth. "Really super! He just, um..." Joy felt her face warm. "Wanted to spend time with his sister."

Devon nodded in understanding, taking his leave. "Well Joy, great seeing you." He glanced at the street to make certain traffic was clear before crossing over. "I'm sure I'll be seeing you around! Noelle comes home next week, I hear."

"That's right!"

"I'll likely be dropping by the inn, then."

"Cool!" Joy said, striding away. "Bye, Devon! Fun running into you!"

Devon held up his hand in a wave.

Then Joy hurried along the freshly shoveled sidewalk, darting around holiday shoppers as she went. Why did she feel sweaty? It was, like, freezing outside! Joy paused to adjust the backpack on her shoulder then barreled ahead, plowing through the blustery snow. The flagpole in the island at the center of the roundabout was just ahead of her, and the post office would be on her left before she reached that. Joy didn't have to read the snow-dusted town sign beside the towering flagpole to know what it said. She'd lived here her whole life. Well, at least until recently. And, the prophetic town motto was etched in her memory:

Welcome to Christmas Town, Tennessee...
Where everyday dreams come true!

They'd certainly come true for lots of people here. But Joy's dreams weren't tied to Christmas Town. They resided across the Atlantic. Far away, in Italy.

Chapter Two

DEVON WATCHED JOY walk away with a dull ache in his heart. That's what running into your old girlfriend would do to you, he supposed. Though it had been two and a half years since they'd broken up, in some ways, Devon hadn't totally gotten Joy out of his system. First love and all that. And, Joy Christmas's appeal hadn't lessened over time; in many ways, she'd gotten better. Even more self-confident and mature. Not to mention, extremely talented. *Oh, yeah. And, also committed to another guy.*

Devon prepared to cross the street to the coffee shop and something odd caught his eye. The flap on Joy's backpack had flipped open and a couple of letters had slipped out—fluttering through the snowy air! Devon gawked in disbelief, as another letter emerged, and then another... Suddenly, a swirl of mail spiraled out behind Joy as she sauntered along, evidently failing to notice. Devon called out to her, but she didn't hear him above the wind. It blew fiercely, shrieking down the sidewalk and sending the strange cache of letters twirling skyward like they were caught up in a snow-speckled, mini tornado! Holiday shoppers turned to stare as Devon dashed down the sidewalk, leaping after the errant mail. *There!* He snagged one. *Aha!* And, yet another! A third letter bounced off the shoulder of a surprised woman's coat and Devon nabbed it quickly.

"Joy!" Devon called breathlessly, chasing after her. "Joy Christmas!"

She turned with alarm just as she reached the short row of mailboxes lining the sidewalk in front of the post office. "Devon?"

He jogged her way, a clutch of letters in his hands. "These fell out of your backpack!" he said, thinking it had actually looked more like they'd flown. But that sounded so crazy, Devon decided not to mention it.

Joy's brow rose. "What?"

"These," Devon said, handing the mail to her. "They were just... I mean, the flap of your backpack must have come open."

She slid it off her shoulder and stared into its open hollow. "Gosh! You're right!"

Several other letters were nestled inside, but they appeared a bit restless to Devon's eye. *But letters don't jiggle on their own*, Devon told himself rationally. Those envelopes were simply shifting into place after Joy had lowered her backpack.

Devon handed Joy the letters he'd grabbed, and she sifted through them. "These are the ones going to folks in town," she said, eyeing the cards addressed to her grandparents, uncles and aunts, and distant relatives. "Family members!"

"The Christmases and the Clauses?" Devon asked, having watched Joy sort the letters.

"Yeah. Weird."

When Joy looked up and fixed him with her gorgeous blue eyes, Devon's heart thumped. A pretty blush swept her creamy complexion and long blond hair spilled from beneath her hat, grazing the tops of her coat's arms. At five foot ten Joy was nearly as tall as he was. When she wore boots with heels, as she often did, she and Devon were about even. Without meaning to, Devon recalled how easy it had been to take her in his arms and kiss her back then. Back when they'd been a couple. Inseparable and in love.

"Those must have been the ones on top," Devon told her. He hated the fact that his voice sounded kind of scratchy.

"Hmm. Maybe?" Joy seemed to consider this. Then, she stuffed those letters into a street-side mailbox, along with the others from her pack. "Well, anyway!" she said brightly. "Thanks for rescuing my mail! Dad and Gloria would have been sad if all their letters hadn't gotten delivered."

"That, and some folks in town might have felt slighted." Devon chuckled, thinking of Joy's quirky grandparents, Lou and Buddy Christmas, as well as the other members of her family. They were all a warm bunch, but a little on the eccentric side. Then again, Devon's parents were a bit offbeat, too. They were both artists, specializing in ceramics, and not ultra conventional. Neither was Devon, when he thought of it. He enjoyed doing his own thing, and didn't much care what others thought about it. At least, he hadn't cared in quite a while.

"True that!" Joy rolled her eyes and the back of Devon's neck warmed. That was one of her little habits that had always gotten to him: that super cute eye-roll. It was a good thing Devon didn't run into Joy more often. Because, being with her today was starting to bring back memories. And that wasn't good. Because Joy had a boyfriend. Supposedly. Although, where was the guy anyhow, if his relationship with Joy was so all-important?

"Well, anyway!" Joy said, turning back toward the Grand Hotel. "Thanks again!"

Since they were both headed in the same direction, Devon decided to walk with her. As they passed the Holly and the Ivy home goods store, Devon caught their joint reflection in the big front window and experienced an uncanny déjà vu. Once, when they were in high school, he and Joy had walked down to the courthouse to deliver something to Sheriff Livingston for Joy's grandma, Lou, who was also the mayor. After running their errand, Joy had hurried down the courthouse steps and scampered into the roundabout facing it. Devon had yelled at her for dashing across the street like that, but she'd laughed and said she'd checked to be sure no cars were coming. Joy had led Devon to the town sign then, the one that said that thing about dreams coming true.

"What do you think, Devon?" she'd asked, giving him a sassy stare. "Will it happen?"

Devon hadn't been totally sure what she was hinting at, but he'd surmised she was asking him if they might have a future. That was the first time that he'd kissed her. Right there in the middle of the roundabout with snow falling down all around them.

"Earth to Devon, hey!" Joy nudged him with a giggle, and Devon realized he'd slipped away.

"You still going to Jolly Bean Java?" she asked. "Or, what?"

Devon stared in surprise, seeing they were right across the street from it.

"Oh, yeah! Ha! Sorry." He shook his head. "Just remembering something."

Joy shot him an inquisitive look and Devon's pulse raced. He definitely wasn't telling her about that memory.

"Something about my workshop," he lied.

"It's cool you've got your own studio now."

"I like it."

Joy cocked her chin to study him. "You're very good at what you do."

"So are you," Devon said, easily returning her compliment. It was time for Joy to walk away, but, interestingly, she seemed the slightest bit hesitant about departing. Devon found himself reluctant to leave Joy's company, too. It had been eons since the two of them had just sat and talked. There was so much to catch up on, and they were both adults now. No reason they couldn't—

"Maybe we should catch up sometime?" she said, before Devon could broach it. "Grab a coffee, or something?"

"That would be..." He swallowed past the lump in his throat. "Great!"

"You can tell me what you're working on, and I'll fill you in on my life in Italy!" Joy's eyes sparkled merrily, and Devon wondered if he'd made a tactical error. He'd thought he was over Joy. Way over his feelings for her. Now, he found himself starting to wonder how true that was.

"When and where?"

"I'm watching Xavier for my folks in the morning. Gloria's working on a production at the children's theater, and Dad's helping Olivia and Nick with some stuff at Sleigh Bell Stables." Joy's smile brightened. "But, I'm free in the afternoon!"

"Want to say three, then?"

"Three sounds good."

Devon's gaze darted across the road. "Jolly Bean Java?"

"Er..." She hedged and Devon got why. He and Joy had hung out together at Jolly Bean Java all the time as a teenage couple. Maybe another spot would prove better for reconnecting. On a purely platonic level. Which this was. Platonic. Purely. Even though, now that he'd remembered it, Devon was finding it hard to forget about his and Joy's first kiss. Joy's lips had been soft, wonderful, and warm—as she'd wound her arms around him. "How about the café at the Elf Shelf Bookshop? I hear their scones are really good."

"I *love* scones," Devon said, his tone unintentionally husky.

Joy gave him a bemused smile. "Yeah. Me, too."

Chapter Three

THE NEXT DAY, Joy spent a happy morning getting to know her little brother, Xavier. The sunny-natured baby had dark hair and eyes, and alabaster skin. His big, goofy grin revealed that his lower two middle teeth had come in. From the way he chomped on his candy-cane-striped teething ring, Joy guessed that additional teeth were on their way. She sat with Xavier on his play blanket near the Christmas tree in the library at the Christmas Inn. At six months old, Xavier was big enough to sit steadily on his own, but he wasn't quite crawling yet, which meant it was easy to keep him out of mischief. Joy had been reading the family favorite from a library bookshelf: *The Night Before Christmas* by Clement C. Moore. Xavier had gurgled excitedly as Joy turned the colorful pages. Then, he'd dropped his teething ring and clapped his chubby hands together when Joy read the last line. Santa and his reindeer team rode off into the night sky with Santa wishing all a happy Christmas and a good night.

Joy had always loved this story herself, but it resonated even more sweetly when she found herself reading it to a baby. "Come here, you," she said, reaching for the chubby infant. Joy lifted Xavier into her lap and held the small boy close. He smelled of baby powder freshness and applesauce, Joy thought with a giggle. A tad like Christmas cookies, too... That latter scent reminded Joy of her dad, Walt, who was such a big fan of the holiday—and cookies. Left unchecked, he'd likely eat them nonstop. Fortunately, Walt now had Gloria to keep him in line. Which was a great thing, since both Joy and Noelle had moved away.

Joy studied the five stockings hanging from the mantel and felt a sudden tug at her heartstrings. Two of the stockings were very old, but still in good shape. They contained reindeer designs and were each very slightly different, with the major difference being the addition of the girls' individual names. They'd been handmade for Joy and Noelle by their late mother, Rose, when the twins were newborns. Two others, with an elegant hand-stitched poinsettia design, were identically matching. Joy and Noelle had given those to Gloria and Walt as Christmas presents when Gloria first joined their family. The final stocking, with a darling hobbyhorse on it, was labeled "Xavier."

Joy hated that she hadn't been here for Xavier's birth. While Noelle hadn't been here on the actual day of the delivery, she'd driven home from school at the first opportunity, which was the following weekend. Joy had missed other things, too. Like her Grandpa Buddy's fall in September, though he was thankfully doing much better now. Then, there was the awesome news relating to Gloria's brother, Joy's Uncle David. He and Liz Martin had very recently become engaged. While Joy was so happy for them, she was already fretting over how to finance her travel expenses for their wedding. After making a big stink about being an independent adult in Italy, Joy didn't want to go begging to her dad and Gloria for a plane ticket. She supposed, if she invited Giacomo, he might offer to foot the bill, but that didn't sit well with Joy, either.

She wasn't sure whether it was the idea of including Giacomo at her uncle's wedding, or him paying for her ticket that made Joy feel worse. In the end, she decided it was both things. She and Giacomo hadn't parted on the best terms, and now Joy was wondering whether she was really meant to be with him at all. Naturally, she understood his reasons for wanting to stay in Italy this Christmas. But, what about next year? Would they have to work out some sort of rotation, in fairness to them both and their corresponding families? Joy hugged Xavier tighter, knowing it would only get more complicated, should she and Giacomo eventually decide to marry and have kids. She tried to envision chasing little bilingual babies through a piazza in Florence, but the images came out all fuzzy. Was that really what Joy wanted? To stay in Italy forever?

She and Giacomo hadn't discussed the far future in much detail. They'd only focused on goals close at hand, like him getting through his professional architectural studies. *Then*, he'd told her lovingly, wrapping his strong arms around her, *we'll have so many choices*. Yeah, but like what? Somehow Joy didn't imagine that one of those "choices" would involve the couple relocating to Christmas Town. Giacomo was far too cosmopolitan for that. Plus, he'd grown accustomed to a certain lifestyle. The sort of life his parents led, and which he'd intimated he'd like to emulate one day for his own family.

Joy sighed heavily and kissed the top of Xavier's head, as he snuggled back against her. The baby was growing weighty and, she realized, looking a little sleepy-headed, too. The lulling flames of the hearth across the way crackled softly, as Joy hugged the baby to her and studied her favorite room at the Christmas Inn. It contained cozy yet elegant furnishings, including two seating areas, with one facing the fireplace and another in a back corner of the room. Her dad's rolltop desk was in here, and also a freestanding cabinet used as a bar. So was the toy box Grandpa Buddy had built for her and Noelle when they were small.

Dark paneled walls held bookshelves teeming with numerous tomes—on all the topics in the world! Her dad was such a reader, and loved geography, too. When Noelle and Joy were small, Walt used every opportunity to bring his big globe on a stand into their conversations, by pointing out whichever place he was talking about on the richly decorated tan and brown orb. Walt had a special affinity for the Maritime Provinces in Canada, which, he always told the girls, was a very special family place. They still had distant relatives living there on the Claus side. Every once in a while, Walt hinted at magical happenings there, and his blue eyes would twinkle. This would cause Joy and Noelle to squeal with delight and beg their daddy to take them to see the reindeer. Yet, his response was the same every time. Walt would deeply chuckle and say, *Not just yet.*

Xavier sagged further in Joy's arms, and she decided it was time to put him down for his morning nap. He was such a good child and so easy to care for. The little tyke made her dad and Gloria awfully happy, too, and Joy was elated to see them both so content and in love. Joy's dad deserved love. Walt was a good man, who'd been a great father. Finally, when Gloria came along, it was time for the longtime widower to grab a bit of happiness for himself. And, Joy and Noelle both had been delighted that he had. Gloria was a very sweet woman, and she was totally awesome for Walt. Gloria was warm and funny, and sometimes a little bossy, but those qualities seemed to suit Joy's dad well, as they complemented aspects of his personality. Joy reflected on her dad and Gloria being the perfect match and wondered how they'd instinctively known they were meant to be together. According to Noelle, who'd been living at the inn that first Christmas when Gloria arrived and began dating their dad, it hadn't taken long for the middle-aged lovebirds to admit—then ultimately act on—their strong feelings for each other.

"Looks like someone's had a busy morning!" Gloria chirped quietly from the threshold to the living room, and Joy saw her standing there with her white hat and coat on.

Joy glanced down at baby Xavier, who'd dozed off in her arms, and chuckled softly. "I was just about to put him down for his nap."

Gloria slipped off her hat and unbuttoned her coat with a soft smile. "No worries. I'll take him upstairs." She swiftly removed her gloves. "Let me just hang up my coat in the hall closet."

"How did things go at the theater?" Joy asked, before Gloria inched away.

"Really super!" Gloria said, beaming. "Savannah and I are one step closer to having that puppet show ready. With the assistance of all our little helpers, of course."

***

"Thanks for watching Xavier," Gloria said a short time later. "It was a big help."

The two women stood in the kitchen, where Joy was helping Gloria prepare lunch: a tomato bisque and grilled portobello mushroom sandwiches, with a leafy green side salad. Walt would be home to join them for the meal at any minute.

"I was happy to do it," Joy said, tossing the greens. "He's such a tiny nugget! So cute! And, sweet!"

"Yeah, Walt and I are lucky." Gloria grinned fondly at the girl. "Three times over, it seems."

Joy had to resist the urge to hug her. Gloria was always saying heartfelt things like that, and the cool thing was she meant them. Gloria's heart was big and warm, and full of love. When she'd fallen for Walt, she hadn't just opened her heart to him; she'd extended her love to his whole family. Now, Walt's family was embracing Gloria's. Her brother David had initially come to Christmas Town as the interim pastor at the Corner Church. Then the coolest thing occurred. He decided to stay here permanently, and marry Liz Martin!

"I'm so excited about Uncle David staying in town," Joy said to Gloria. "And, about him marrying Liz!"

"I know! It's great news. He only told us last week."

"I can't wait to congratulate him," Joy said.

Gloria twinkled her way. "You'll have your chance soon. You dad and I have invited David and Liz over for an engagement celebration dinner on Saturday."

"Nice."

"Noelle will be home by then," Gloria added. "So, we thought we'd include Devon Slade, too."

"Devon?" Joy asked, her head suddenly light.

"That is all right? I ran into him at the Grand Hotel this morning, and asked if he'd like to be included." Gloria viewed her worriedly. "Your dad and I talked about keeping it a family thing, but Noelle and Devon have become so tight, and we thought—"

"No, no!" Joy rushed in. "That sounds fine."

Gloria hesitated a beat. "If it's awkward for you... I mean, I know that you and Devon used to date."

"A long time ago."

Gloria eyed her carefully. "But, since you're with Giacomo now, and Noelle and Devon are just friends—"

"Sure! Yeah! No problem. Seriously." But, if that were the case, then why did Joy's insides feel all squiggly? "I'm cool with Devon being here," she stated boldly, in part to convince herself. "There's no reason that he and I can't be friends, too! Like you say, I've got Giacomo, and...and..."

"Joy?"

"Huh?"

"Sweetheart, you just dunked the salad tongs into the bisque."

Joy stared in horror, seeing that she had. Wilted pieces of dark leafy greens floated on top of the hot tomato soup, looking like shriveled-up foliage. "Oops!"

Joy grimaced and started trying to pick them out with the salad tongs, but they were slick and kept dropping back into the bisque.

"You know what?" Gloria said soothingly. "Why don't you let me do that?"

"Oh gosh, Gloria! I'm so sorry." Joy surrendered the salad tongs with a blush. "I don't know what came over me."

Gloria set a hand on her hip, the tongs poised in her opposite hand. "You're sure this isn't about Devon?"

"Devon? No! He's great. He and I are great! I ran into him yesterday, in fact, and the two of us are going out for coffee, which is..."

Gloria shared a tentative grin. "Great?"

Joy nodded enthusiastically. "Yeah," she said, catching her breath. "That."

"Wonderful!" Gloria's eyebrows rose. "When?"

"Later today. At three o'clock."

"Jolly Bean Java?"

"Elf Shelf."

"Fun."

"Yeah!"

Walt's big voice boomed down the hall as he strode toward the kitchen. "Afternoon, ladies! Guess who's *ho-ho-home*?"

Joy and Gloria spun toward him as he entered the kitchen through the breakfast area, dressed in a flannel shirt and jeans. "*Shh...*" they both said together, but they were giggling. "Xavier's sleeping."

Walt Christmas was a handsome guy in his mid-forties with a full beard and mustache and bright blue eyes, which shone a little brighter ever since he'd married Gloria. "I'll be sure to keep my voice down," he said in a whisper. Walt's gaze took in the lunch fixings. "Something smells delicious."

Gloria grinned at her husband. "It will be ready in a jiff."

"Can I do something to help?"

"Set the table, maybe?"

"That's all right, I'll do it," Joy offered helpfully, mostly because she wanted to distance herself from the mess she'd made with the soup.

Chapter Four

LATER THAT AFTERNOON, Devon sat across from Joy at the bookstore café. They'd just grabbed an empty table and both had removed their coats. When Devon tugged off his hat, Joy shouted, "Whoa!" Then she lowered her voice, when she realized how loud she'd been. "You cut it?"

Devon raked a hand through his short dark hair, which was about as dark brown as hair could get before being black. "Yeah." From his senior year in high school until just last spring, he'd worn it shoulder-length and pulled back in a ponytail. "I decided it was time."

"What? When?"

About the time you ran off to Italy with what's-his-name, Devon thought, but didn't say. Instead, he offered up a vague reply. "Not sure, exactly."

"So, you just, what?" Joy gaped in disbelief. "Walked into the Candy Cane Barbershop, and said 'I want a new look'?"

Devon chuckled at her guess, which was actually fairly accurate. "Something like that."

"Because?"

Devon twinkled her way, then teased, "I thought this look was more manly."

"I'd say the other way was plenty manly enough."

Devon's stomach flipped because that sounded kind of flirty.

"Not that this way's not good, too!" Joy amended quickly.

"That's one heck of a lot of 'nots,'" Devon joked, feeling his gut clench.

Joy squared her narrow shoulders. "The English is a little rusty," she quipped, sitting up straighter.

"You couldn't have lost it all so soon."

"Nope! That's true. I give some of my tours in English."

"Yeah? How's that going?"

"Good! Pretty good!"

"And, your painting...?"

"Fabulous, too."

Devon stopped himself from asking about the boyfriend, because—honestly—he didn't want to know. He'd already heard Joy sing the guy's praises once, and that was certainly enough. Devon peered toward the coffee counter. "What would you like? I'll grab us something."

"Oh, no. You don't have to—"

"Come on." He locked on her gaze. "I'm employed now. I can afford it."

"You've always been employed, as long as I've known you. First, at your parents' shop. Then, at Jolly Bean Java."

"I was the best barista in town," Devon joked. "Until Mr. Smith came along." He leaned toward Joy, then said teasingly, "And, also maybe the handsomest?"

"Devon Slade!" Joy's pretty mouth dropped open. "I can't believe you! You're fishing."

Devon's fingers drummed the table. "Always thought there was a reason all those ladies came around. One double-shot latte after the other."

"You really are incorrigible."

Devon's brow shot up. "You're saying it's not true?"

Joy thumbed her chest then admitted with a chuckle, "Okay. All right. Maybe *I* came around time after time, but that was different." She defiantly met his eyes. "We were dating. Or, about to be, anyway."

"I've never seen a girl drink so much coffee."

"I had to get your attention somehow," she said with a sassy twang.

"Don't worry," he said. "You had it."

Electricity sizzled between them as Joy stared into his eyes. After a minute, she said, "Coffee! Yeah! I'll take a..." Devon leaned toward her and she flushed. "You know what I like." Joy admitted the next part shyly, which Devon found endearing. "The truth is they're kind of tough to get in Italy. Everything's hardcore. Espresso, or the café au lait kind of deal."

"Ah. No caramel macchiatos there, I suppose?"

"Not a one!"

"Peppermint mochas?"

"I honestly haven't looked, but I doubt it."

Devon was about to ask what she found so great about Florence, but he didn't. Mostly because he was scared that the answer contained the initials G. and R.

Devon pushed back his chair and stood, preparing to get their coffees. "Would you like one of those scones we talked about?"

Joy thought on this, looking tempted. "Maybe some other time? I had an awfully big lunch."

"Okay," Devon returned easily. "Be back in a flash."

***

Devon swore he was gone less than five minutes, but that must have been long enough for Joy to set up her surprise. He returned to their table catching Joy scrolling through something on her phone.

"Oh, sorry!" she said, looking up. "That was just Noelle texting, saying sheeeee..... Eeek!" Joy's voice rose in a screech as she surveyed the brimming plate of oatmeal raisin cookies that had appeared on their table. "Wha...what's all this?"

Devon set their coffee cups down and took his seat, scanning the table. "Looks like a whole lot of oatmeal cookies! Maybe two dozen?" His gaze snagged on two pint-size cartons beside the loaded platter, which was covered with green holiday plastic wrap and crowned with a big red bow. The small milk cartons were the individual-size sort sold in school cafeterias. "Whoa, Joy." He eyed her admiringly. "What a very unexpected gift!"

"No...I... What I mean is... Well!" She paused to suck in a gasp then simply said, "Gosh," her eyes growing wide.

"I don't know what to say," Devon told her.

"That makes two of us, yeah."

Devon passed Joy her coffee and she gripped the cup firmly.

"I didn't even see any of that when you came in," he said in amazement. "Where were you hiding things? In your purse?"

"Hmm." Joy glanced down at her bulky shoulder bag and grimaced tightly. "Maybe?"

Devon took a sip from his cup, surveying her. "That was awfully sweet of you to remember. Oatmeal raisin are my favorite kind."

"Now that you mention it, you're right!"

"Now that I...?" Devon shook his head. "These are a gift from you, right? Something that you baked me? Maybe as a little peace offering?"

"Peace offering?" she asked anxiously. "What do you mean?"

"For how things ended. You know." Devon shrugged blandly, feigning indifference. "Between us back then."

"Between us?" she asked, thrown. "It was a mutual—"

"Oh really?"

She considered this a moment, her blue eyes glistening. "Wasn't it?"

"On your end, maybe."

"That's not what *mutual* means."

"There's another 'not.'"

"Stop trying to throw the conversation off track, Devon."

"I'm not."

"Ha-ha!" She sat back in her chair, and then gasped. "Oh. My. Gosh. *No*." Joy blinked in understanding. "You didn't want to?"

"Break up?" he replied. "Nope."

"But, you said—"

"I wasn't going to hold you back, Joy." Though it hurt to admit the truth, Devon decided she had the right to know. "You were headed to Europe. Going places... Just look at you now! Living in Italy, wow!"

Devon recalled that stupid poster his parents kept in the kiln room. It had a seagull on it, and said something about letting free the things you loved. If they loved you back, they'd always come home to you. Such a big, stinking lie... When he was younger, though, Devon had believed it. He'd been naïve then. Time had changed him. These past few years had changed him. But apparently not his heart, in a way. Because, weirdly, it still felt bruised when he looked in Joy's eyes. Still, Devon knew he'd done the right thing for Joy, and probably for them both. Look where he was now! A practicing artist with his own woodworking studio... Which was very, very cool.

"Italy. Wow." Joy repeated his words a little sadly then slowly looked up. "I'm sorry, Devon. I really didn't know. It was hard for me, too. But, when I thought that's what you wanted also, I—"

"Joy," he said kindly. "Ancient history. All right?"

"You're sure?"

"Sure, I'm sure."

"Water under the bridge?"

"And, over the dam," Devon assured her, because that's what he needed her to believe. Then, to prove it, he decided to ask about Mr. Italy. "So!" Devon said, sipping from his cup. "How's Gelato?"

"Giacomo," Joy corrected, but she was giggling. "Gosh, Devon."

"Romesco?"

Joy twisted her lips. "Romano."

"Right."

"Gelato's a type of ice cream and romesco's a sauce." She gave that charming eye-roll and Devon's neck warmed. "Giacomo Romano is a *man*."

Yeah, and a pretty buff one, from what Devon had seen. Not that Devon didn't keep himself in shape. *"Not." "Not." "Not"... Argh.* "Exactly so," Devon said smartly. "And, studying to be an architect, yeah?"

"Yeah!"

"When will he be done?"

"With his studies? Soon, we hope. Probably by the end of this year."

"And, then?"

Joy squirmed in her chair. "We...haven't actually talked about it."

"Huh." Devon studied her a beat and a blush swept her cheeks. "Well, I guess that you've got time."

"*Months*. Yeah." She surveyed the cookies on the table, appearing baffled. Next, she met Devon's eyes, introducing a new topic. "Tell me about your studio?"

And so, Devon did. As he and Joy spoke, each of them grew more comfortable with their conversation. Joy talked about being a docent, and the unusual and funny tour groups she sometimes led, and told Devon all about Florence and a nearby town which she loved, called Fiesole.

Before they knew it, two hours had passed, and the sky had turned pitch-black outdoors. Small dots of white darted past the bookstore's front window, which held a display showcasing a small wooden train on a track and a toy Santa with a tiny hammer, which bobbed back and forth over a miniature sawhorse holding fake boards.

"Whoa," Devon said, astounded. "How did it get to be five?"

Joy viewed him with wonder. "Gosh! I don't know."

"I should probably get back to that studio I told you so much about," Devon said, chuckling. "We close up at six, and I'll need to take care of some things."

"Of course!" Joy appeared to gather her wits. "And, I...need to stop by the market. I told Gloria and Dad I'd pick up some fresh bread for dinner."

Devon beamed down at their table and the plate full of cookies. "Looks like I'm all set for dessert!"

"Ha."

"Not sure about this milk though," Devon said concernedly. "It has been sitting out a while." He lifted one of the small cartons, and mysteriously found it icy cold. "Well, what do you know? It still feels chilled!"

"What? Really?"

"That's something."

"Uh-huh!" Joy's eyebrows knitted together, like she was working out a puzzle. "Really something!"

"Well, Joy," Devon said, as they both got to their feet. "It's been fun."

"Sure has," she returned sweetly.

"You'll have to drop by my studio sometime."

"I'm headed to the Grand Hotel on Wednesday."

"For Savannah's puppet show?"

"Yeah, that's right. Will you be around?"

"I will," he said, feeling chipper. "Hope to see you then." Devon slipped on his coat and tugged on his hat, before shoving each one of the small milk cartons in a separate coat pocket. Joy's unexpected gift had been incredibly sweet and nostalgic. When they were going out in high school, she used to bake him oatmeal cookies all the time. "And, oh," he said, genuinely touched. "Thanks for the cookies and milk."

Chapter Five

JOY'S HEART HAMMERED as she walked back to the Christmas Inn. That whole milk and cookies thing was so weird. She'd have to talk to her dad about it. He'd know what to do. Walt always did, which was one reason Joy had missed seeing him so much while living in Italy. Even though she was a grown woman now, Joy still sometimes relied upon her dad for advice. And, she definitely needed his advice today.

"Hello?" Joy called, stepping through the front door. "Anybody home?"

"Back here in the library, sweetheart," came her dad's steady reply.

Joy strode that way, noting the rest of the inn seemed quiet. Then she heard Gloria's lighthearted laughter spilling down the front hall from the kitchen, and realized she was coddling Xavier. Likely, talking to him encouragingly as she fed the baby his dinner.

Gitana loped into the living room to greet Joy as she headed to the library. The dog appeared sleepy-eyed, and Joy guessed the yellow Lab had probably been snoozing by the fire in the library while keeping Walt company. Joy found her dad seated in a wing chair by the hearth, a book in hand.

"Welcome back," Walt said, smiling pleasantly. "How was coffee?"

"Great!" For the life of her, Joy swore her dad had something in his mouth. Her gaze dropped to the candy dish on the table near his elbow, seeing half its stash of white peppermint bark had been eaten down.

"Dad!" Joy said disappointedly. "Snacking? Again?"

Walt swallowed hard and coughed into his hand. "Just had one little piece, Joy."

"If you say so." Joy rolled her eyes and chuckled. "Just don't let it ruin your supper. Gloria would be unhappy about that."

"Yes, well." Walt's blue eyes sparkled in collusion. "No need to tell her."

"I'm surprised you haven't gained weight," Joy said, marveling at the fact that her dad looked fitter than ever.

"Well, now... I do work out. And, also get plenty of exercise between looking after Xavier and tending to the inn. Even with Gloria here to help me!"

"Right."

"Is everything okay?" Walt asked concernedly, seeing Joy was still wearing her coat.

"Yeah... No!" Joy stopped talking and sat down in the wing chair facing his. "I just...er...kind of wanted to ask you about something?"

"Ask away!" Walt encouraged warmly as Gitana settled down again, stretching out on the carpet by his feet.

"You know that thing with the cookies?"

"Cookies?" Walt's panicked gaze swept the room, then he met Joy's eyes, appearing oddly called out. "What? Where?"

"Not here." Joy dropped her voice in a whisper. "I was talking about that thing that used to happen." She leaned toward him, resting her elbows on her knees. In addition to her coat, Joy still wore her hat and mittens. "You know, when I was in high school?"

Walt nodded with slow understanding. "This has to do with Devon, doesn't it?" he asked hoarsely.

"I don't know," Joy answered, stymied. "Does it?"

Walt darted a glance toward the door that led to the hall and then the kitchen. "Why don't you tell me what happened? Was it something today?"

"Yes. Dad." Joy grew animated with the telling. "It was so, so weird! I met Devon at the Elf Shelf Bookshop café. Just coffee...an old-friends thing. The next thing I knew he was grabbing our coffees, then—*wham*—there they were!"

Walt's forehead rose. "'Wham'?"

"Yeah," Joy whispered huskily. "A big, brimming platter of oatmeal raisin cookies. Devon's favorite kind."

Walt thoughtfully stroked his beard. "Was there milk involved?"

"Cafeteria milk, but still..."

"Icy cold?"

"Yes!"

Walt whistled through his teeth, catching Joy off guard. "That used to happen, all right." He quizzically viewed his daughter. "I thought you'd outgrown it. Or..."

"You told me not to worry! That the cookies and milk thing would stop happening! And, once I went off to college, it pretty much did."

Walt briefly scanned the stockings hanging from the mantel. "Huh."

"It was freaky, you know," Joy went on. "Being able to conjure up Devon's favorite treat without even trying. You told me it had something to do with my feelings for him. And something about our family and 'Christmas magic.' But, you promised—*promised*—it would all go away!"

"Now, daughter. I didn't precisely say that."

"I want to know what's going on, Dad. And, I mean now."

"Right-this-second now? Or, like, in-the-near-future now?"

Joy huffed in frustration. "How about yesterday?"

Walt uncomfortably cleared his throat. "Right. Right. I see your point."

"Am I cursed somehow? Afflicted?"

Her dad appeared startled and perhaps a bit wounded. "Cursed? Afflicted? Heavens, no!"

"Then, why did this happen again today?"

"Hmm, yes…" Walt scrutinized her a long beat and Joy flushed. "Why did it?" He studied her another few moments before proceeding carefully. "Do you still have feelings for Devon?"

"Me? No. Gosh, no, Dad. That would be silly. Ridiculous. Ha-ha! I'm with Giacomo now! In Florence! Hey! And, we're deliriously happy! So happy you wouldn't believe it! I mean, everyone who sees us is like, 'Wow! You're such a cute couple and so deliriously happy!' I mean, they say that in Italian usually, but the sentiment's the same. Because, well. It's obvious!"

Walt's eyebrows arched. "A simple 'no' would have sufficed, Joy."

Joy bit her bottom lip. "Oh yeah. Sorry."

"Have you noticed anything else unusual?" her dad asked, a non sequitur Joy found hard to follow.

"What do you mean?"

"Since returning to Christmas Town?"

"I only got here on Sunday."

"Forty-eight hours is long enough."

"For what?"

"You didn't answer my question."

Joy pondered it, but so far her return home had seemed routine. Apart from meeting Xavier for the first time, and bumping into Devon when she was delivering... "Wait a minute! The letters!"

Walt sat up straighter at this. "Which letters?"

"The Christmas cards you and Gloria asked me to mail from the post office."

"Yeah. What about them?"

Joy shook her head. "It's probably nothing."

"Why don't you let me be the judge?"

"Well," Joy said a tad nervously. "They were just in my backpack, and it was snowing a lot. Then again, it always does here. And the wind was pretty strong."

"Like it often is here..." Walt said leadingly.

"Yeah! And then I bumped into Devon by the Grand Hotel. And we chatted a bit. Then, I continued down the sidewalk and Devon stopped me."

"Why?"

"He came chasing after me with a handful of letters that had blown right out of my backpack—"

"Blown or flown?" Walt mumbled under his breath.

"The flap must have come open, and..." Joy halted suddenly to gape at her dad. "What do you mean, 'blown or flown'?"

"Who were the letters addressed to?"

"What?" Joy blinked hard. "The Christmases, I guess. And, the Clauses. Pretty much our family and relatives in town."

"This is all very unusual." Walt strummed his fingers against the armrest on his wing chair. "Given that you and Devon are no longer..." His eyes widened at Joy. "Are you?"

"No! Gosh, no!"

"Well, if you're not involved with Devon, and you truly love Giacomo—"

"Love?" Joy's voice came out in a squeak, in spite of herself.

"I thought you said that you did?" Walt asked with a confused stare. "When you decided to move to Italy, you told me and Gloria—"

"Of course! Yeah! I know. And, that was really how I was feeling at the time. Honestly, it's true."

Walt softened his tone and gazed compassionately at his daughter. "And, now?"

Joy hung her head as the weight of the truth hit her. "I really don't know."

"What's changed?"

"Nothing. Everything." Joy sighed heavily. "I'm not exactly sure." Heat prickled the backs of her eyes as she addressed her father. "Giacomo didn't want to come home for Christmas," Joy said, starting to blubber. "Not to Christmas Town."

Walt leapt to his feet when tears sprung to her eyes.

"He said he had *his* family. But, what about *mine*?" Joy's voice cracked, and she whined, "*What about Xavier?*"

"Aww, hon." Walt held his arms open wide and Joy stood on shaky knees and stepped into them. If there was anything Joy hated admitting, it was that she might have been wrong. Wrong about Giacomo... Wrong about Florence... Wrong about leaving Christmas Town, and her family...

Walt hugged her firmly as she wept against his shoulder. "There, there..." he said, tenderly patting her back. "You're not expected to know everything yet."

She pulled back to stare at him teary-eyed, and Walt smiled softly.

"You're only twenty-three, sweetheart. There's so much of your life you still need to figure out."

"And, I'm making a big mess of it," Joy whimpered feebly. "Aren't I?"

Walt tugged a hanky from his hip pocket and handed it to her. "Not at all," he said, while she wiped her cheeks. "For some of us it takes years. Figuring this whole love thing out."

At that moment, Gloria appeared in the hall doorway with Xavier on her hip. "You're home!" she said sweetly to Joy, before noting the mood in the room. Also, likely the streaks of mascara down Joy's cheeks. "Oh, honey," Gloria asked worriedly, "is something wrong?"

"We were just having a little chat," Walt told her. He shot Gloria a telling look. "About family stuff."

"In that case," Gloria said demurely. "Now might be the right time for Xavier's bath." She pinched his chubby cheek and Xavier gurgled happily. "Dinner's at seven," she told them both before leaving. "In the meantime, help yourselves to some wine. I left a bottle of red breathing on the kitchen counter."

When she departed, Walt asked Joy if she'd like a glass, and she said maybe in a bit.

"So?" Joy asked, staring up at her dad. "Are you going to tell me about those flying letters, or what?"

"How about we hang up your coat, first?" he asked kindly.

"Then, we'll talk?"

"Yes."

"And, you'll finally answer my questions? About our family history, and everything?"

"I think you're right, Joy. Now's a good time."

Chapter Six

JOY NERVOUSLY TRAIPSED up the stairs of the Grand Hotel, making her way to the third floor where Devon had his studio. She'd told him she'd stop by, and she still wanted to. Even though her head was swimming from the information her dad had unloaded on her. Joy had always known her family was special; she simply hadn't grasped how truly remarkable their ancestors were. The Christmas and Claus families were related, and their distant-past connections still affected members of each clan today. Certain magical abilities had been passed down from one generation to the next through the family DNA. Yet, a certain element of Christmas or Claus magic was that it had to remain a secret from the general population.

If too many ordinary people were let in on the family secrets, then the Christmas and Claus family magic would eventually cease to work. For magic was more about what folks couldn't see than about what they could prove was real. Magic, as her dad Walt explained it, was largely a measure of faith. The belief in the impossible, and something grander and more beautiful than what people normally expect to find in the everyday world... A universal truth that binds humanity together via its element of hope...

The Christmases and the Clauses weren't cursed. In fact, they were blessed with many special gifts. Sandy Winchester's and Nick Claus's grandparents, who lived in the Maritime Provinces, were the most gifted of all. They brought a special brand of magic to the world each year at Christmastime, one that enlivened the hearts of grown-ups and kids alike with childlike whimsy and the appreciation of the fantastic.

Joy had sensed this all along, but had never concretely believed it to be true. And yet, each time she'd passed the Snow Globe Gallery and had occasion to study the gorgeous snow globe on display in the front window there, Joy had intuited there was a greater truth that she suspected, but wasn't entirely aware of.

The snow globe showcased a mystical scene including a tiny snow-covered cottage next to a barn, rimmed with fir trees. Prancing reindeer stood on the lawn, hitched up to a toy-laden sleigh, and smoke seemed to curl from the tiny home's chimney. The object was a marvel to behold, particularly since—from time to time—its interior looked different, as if the small parts of it had moved around on their own accord. And the fact was, they had. For the snow globe wasn't simply a cheery holiday ornament; it was secretly a closed-circuit television view of life in what family members referred to surreptitiously as the "N. P."

Nick's sister, Sandy Claus Winchester, ran the gallery, and she'd befriended Joy early on, feeling a certain camaraderie with her, as they both were artists. Joy had a special talent with painting, but it was more than that. Her art came so easily to her that her renderings often seemed more than inspired. At times, they felt *magical.* Now Joy understood that being an artist was not just a natural gift; it was a family "gift" as well. Joy had other family talents, too. She could will cookies and milk to appear, and cause mail addressed to the Christmases or the Clauses to float on its own to the N. P., which was actually in the Maritime Provinces—but nobody was supposed to know. The precise location was a heavily guarded secret.

More secrets were kept among the family, with family members even concealing the nature of their particular abilities from others they were close to. Too much exposure to the truth would destroy the magic, and no one wanted to risk causing another relative to lose their special talents. There was only one exception, and that concerned true love. When a Christmas or a Claus found the person they were fated to be with romantically forever, it was not only important that they share the truth with that individual—it was imperative. Otherwise, their bond would be based on false pretenses and the union wouldn't last.

Telling someone you love that your family is a "little unusual" can be draining and uncomfortable, her dad had said. But in the end, of course, so totally worth it. He'd had a heart-to-heart with Gloria, and before that with Joy and Noelle's mom, Rose, long ago. Someday, when the timing was right for Joy, she would be faced with mastering her own unique abilities. She would also need to discuss them with her potential life's mate.

Joy tried to imagine the look in Giacomo's eyes if she started to fill him in on her family secrets. Would he think that she was out of her mind, or at least headed it that direction? Joy found herself silently wondering if Devon might take the news differently. Devon had grown up in Christmas Town. Perhaps he'd already caught a glimmer of something. Had he wondered when they were dating about those mysteriously appearing cookies and milk? Joy hadn't told him the truth then, and wasn't exactly prepared to now. And, anyway, it certainly wasn't merited, since she and Devon were simply friends, and he wasn't her destined partner, or anything like that.

"Why, Joy Christmas!" a cheerful female voice called. "Aren't you a sight for sore eyes?"

Joy looked across the top of the landing to see Liz Martin greeting her merrily. Early-forties Liz was tall and slim with long curly brown hair and twinkling brown eyes. Cute dimples settled on either side of her mouth when she smiled. Liz stood in the doorway to her artist studio, wearing a short green apron and a big, bold grin. "I heard you were back in Christmas Town. Welcome home!"

The women hugged hello, with Joy saying how happy she was to see Liz.

"I hear congratulations are in order," Joy further said in low tones. "You and Uncle David... Yay!"

Liz beamed and held out her hand. "He got me this vintage engagement ring from Miami."

Joy took Liz's hand to admire the antique setting and the lovely solitaire diamond. "Wow. Nice!" She grinned warmly at Liz. "Uncle David has good taste."

"I know," Liz heartily agreed. "I love it."

"I also meant about you."

"Aww, sweetie!" Liz bubbled happily. Then, she hugged Joy again. "Come on in and see my space!"

"Are you going to the puppet show?"

"In a minute." Liz darted a glance at the slow-moving line snaking its way up the steps to the fourth floor. "Want to take a peek at my studio in the meantime?"

"I'd love to."

While Joy had seen Liz's studio when Liz first set it up at the beginning of this year, Liz had made many improvements since then. She now offered twice as many knickknacks, and tons more jewelry. All of them had a Christmas theme, and many were patterned after Hannah Livingston's famous heart-shaped Virginia Cookies. Hannah's cookies were made of gingerbread and other "top secret" ingredients, and each was supposedly imbued with special properties.

Joy lifted a pencil holder that had all three types of cookies on it. "Aww, this is so cute!" Her finger traced the cookie sporting a sweet blond-haired angel dressed in white with shimmering wings and wearing a halo. That was the Charity Cookie, meant to inspire good works. The second cookie with a pretty green Christmas tree on it was said to foster forgiveness, and was called the Clemency Cookie. The third cookie, the Commitment Cookie, was decorated with a pink icing heart and carried the romantic phrase *Forever Yours*. Joy knew all about that type. She'd tried it once, a very long time ago.

"I love it in here," Joy said, glancing around the nicely laid out area. Liz had a worktable at one end near a supply cabinet, and a small office set up with a computer and a cash register in another part of the room. Shelves, glass cases, and jewelry holders had Liz's wares on display, including T-shirts and dishtowels embossed with the Virginia Cookies emblem. "You're stocking so much more stuff now, than before!"

"I'm making so much more stuff now, than before." Liz's smile sparkled. "I have to in order to keep up with my sales."

Joy fondly studied the older woman, who made such a good match for her warmhearted Puerto Rican uncle. "I'm glad to hear business is going so well for you."

"Yeah," Liz agreed giddily. "It's been really fun! Who knew so many people would want to buy barrettes?"

Joy walked over to a pivoting stand to study Liz's darling hair accessories. "Are these the newest editions?" she asked, lightly fingering a trio of Virginia Cookie barrettes mounted together on one sales card.

"They are!"

Joy grinned at Liz. "Then, I'll have to buy myself a set."

Chapter Seven

DEVON HAD JUST about given up on Joy dropping by when she appeared in his doorway. "Hey!" he said, smiling her way. "Good to see you."

"You, too!" She grinned and walked into the studio, glancing around at the various pieces of furniture he'd made, and at his work in progress. Devon had been building a writing desk from quarter-sawn oak with the frame crafted from poplar. Its top was four feet across and two feet deep. The piece was basically put together. He just needed to stain it until it held the right sheen. The writing table was a Christmas gift for Noelle. Devon didn't think Joy would mind him giving such a personal gift to her sister, but he wasn't sure. Joy had been acting a bit differently since returning to Christmas Town.

"Whoa, impressive in here," she said, walking toward him. Joy dragged her hand along the smooth surface of the table and looked up. "This is gorgeous, Devon! Is it a desk?"

"A very specific kind of desk." Devon dusted off his hands and removed his work apron. "It's a writing desk—for Noelle."

"Noelle?"

"A Christmas gift."

Color swept Joy's cheeks. "Oh! Oh, how nice!" She turned and pretended to study the cutting boards arranged on a sale shelf behind her. "I'm sure she'll be thrilled."

"We're just friends, you know."

"Sure!" Joy said over her shoulder.

"Have been for a while."

Joy shrugged and picked up a cutting board, examining it more closely, and Devon stepped toward her.

"Joy," he said, his voice low. "Is something wrong?" But he really didn't have to ask, because Devon already knew it was. Joy got quiet when something was bothering her. And, quiet was very unlike Joy.

Instead of answering, she shook her head, her long blonde ponytail swinging behind her. Joy had removed her hat and mittens, as well as her coat, which she held in a bundle under one arm. She wore slim-cut jeans and a plaid flannel shirt that was fitted and feminine, and which Devon thought he recognized from high school. Devon laid a hand on her arm, and then he wished he hadn't. Because, touching Joy only made him want to hold her, accentuating the ache he felt inside.

"Noelle's very passionate about her writing," he said. "She's great at it, too." He stepped a few inches closer. "Just like you are with your art."

"Yeah, but..." Her voice wavered. "You never built me an easel. Or, anything else, for that matter." She turned to face him and Devon's hand slipped off her arm. He was surprised to find Joy's eyes moist. "Not even when we were dating."

"That's not true." His gaze poured over her and his heart thumped. "I did make you something."

Joy blinked in surprise. "What?"

"A toboggan, Joy," he said huskily. Devon motioned with his chin. "That one in the corner, over there."

She stared at it agape. "But you never said..."

"I started working on it that spring," he explained. "The one when you got your early acceptance to the Florence program. I planned to have it finished by Christmas, and give it to you then."

Joy's shoulders sagged in understanding. "But, we broke up that summer, before I left for Italy."

"When I got this studio space, I found the toboggan lying around in my parents' garage, and I figured I might as well finish it." Devon shrugged. "Otherwise, it was a waste of good wood."

"Devon, gosh..." Remorse was written in her eyes. "I'm sorry."

"It's all right," he said, pushing past his melancholy. "It was probably a stupid gift idea, anyway."

"No, it was an awesome gift," she said emphatically before adding more timidly, "I mean, it would have been." She studied him and Devon was momentarily lost in her pretty blue gaze. "You were always good at presents, as far as I recall. You gave me this beautiful necklace."

To Devon's amazement, Joy dug beneath the V of her open neckline and extracted a thin silver chain. A small charm dangled from it. The charm was shaped like an artist's palette with little hollows of paint in different colors on it. There was even a miniature paintbrush laid across it on one end. Devon was touched, and also a bit bewildered. He'd given that to Joy as her high school graduation gift, many years ago. "You still have that?" he asked, moved. "Wow."

Joy locked on his gaze and Devon wished more than anything that he knew what she was thinking. "I still wear it every day."

"And Giacomo?" Devon had to ask. "Does he know where it came from?"

"Yeah." She laughed a little sadly. "I honestly don't think he cares."

"What do you mean?"

"Only that Giacomo's super confident," Joy responded. "He's not the jealous type, or anything like that."

Well, that made one of them, Devon confided to himself. Because the thought of Joy being with Giacomo still made Devon a little crazy. Which was why he tried hard not to think about it. "He trusts you."

"Yeah, but it's not only that..." To Devon's delighted surprise, Joy's mouth twitched just a little. "It's also because he's cocky."

Devon chuckled out loud. "Got it."

"He can't imagine I'd ever look at any other guy." But, even as she said it, she held Devon in her gaze.

"Devon?"

"Huh?"

"The truth is..." Joy fretfully licked her lips. "That Giacomo and I...er..."

Devon waited, his heart pounding. If she said what he was hoping she would, his heart would explode from happiness. Not for Joy, if it pained her, of course. Nor for Giacomo, either. But, Devon couldn't help how he secretly felt. He wanted for Joy to say that she and Giacomo were no longer an item. "Yes?"

Joy puffed out a breath and then said quietly, "We're kind of taking a break at the moment."

Devon scanned her eyes. "What's a 'break' mean?"

"Momentarily not together," she offered. "Till we figure things out."

"Like?"

"Like whether he and I are meant to be together."

Devon mentally fist-pumped. Outwardly, though, he played it cool. "Oh, wow, Joy. I'm...sorry?"

"It's okay." She smiled softly. "It's good to have some space, I think."

"Space is always good," Devon confirmed with a nod. "And Christmas Town's a great place to find it."

"That's what I think, too." Her blue eyes sparkled, and it was all Devon could do not to hold her. He shoved his hands in his jeans pockets instead.

"So what are your plans for the holiday?"

"Just relaxing." Joy thoughtfully angled her chin. "Hanging around."

"Those sound like good plans," Devon told her. "I'm planning on relaxing, too. And, hanging around."

"What about your studio?"

"It's not open every day. It's closed on Sundays and Mondays. And, also on Christmas Eve and Christmas Day."

"New Year's Eve and New Year's Day, too?"

"Yeah."

Joy smiled up at him and Devon's pulse raced. "You're taking Noelle to the ball, aren't you?"

Devon blanched, not having expected that question. "Well, yeah… I mean, she and I discussed it. As friends, like we've gone before. Joy, I don't want you to think—"

"Devon," she said, stopping him. "It's *o-kay*. I don't mind that you're going to the ball with Noelle."

"No?"

"It's fine! Totally fine!"

"If you're uncomfortable..."

"Why would I be uncomfortable? You took her last year, and the year before!"

"Yeah, but last year, and the year before, you had Giacomo."

Joy's eyes shone when she answered. "I'm honestly not worried about it. Besides," she said sweetly. "Noelle's probably counting on it. There's no reason to disappoint her. I mean..." She shrugged sassily. "It's not like you and are I dating again, or anything."

Devon's neck warmed. "Umm...no."

"So, there! You two go and have a great time."

Devon blinked and stared past her shoulder. "Gee, Joy! You seriously didn't have to. Again."

Her eyebrows knitted, then she spun on her heel to see what he was looking at: an enormous holiday platter of oatmeal raisin cookies that sat on the counter by his cash register. Two small cartons of milk were beside it.

"Though, I did totally enjoy the last ones!" he added quickly. "They were super delicious!"

Joy peered at him in an odd way. "Wait. You've eaten those already?"

"Only half," he assured her. "Okay, maybe a little more than... The truth is, there are only a couple left. They honestly were very, very good, Joy. Some of the best you've ever baked me!"

"Er...great!" she said, looking stunned, probably by the fact that Devon had turned into such a huge glutton. He normally didn't overindulge that way, but something about that latest batch of Joy's cookies had seemed different. He absolutely hadn't been able to resist them.

Joy peeked into the empty hallway, seeing the line to the fourth floor had disappeared up the steps and that the surrounding studios had closed up shop, with their front windows darkened. "I guess I'd better get up to that puppet show before it starts."

"Good idea."

"Thanks for showing me your studio!"

"Any time." As she turned toward the door, he said, "Thanks so much for the cookies. And, uh...milk!"

Joy flushed brilliantly and echoed, "Any time!"

Before she completely slipped away, Devon called out to her. "Hey, Joy!"

She turned with a hopeful blush. "Yeah?"

"We should hang out sometime."

"Gloria said you're coming to the house on Saturday for dinner."

Devon nodded. "I meant, other than that."

"Hanging out would be good!"

"What are you up for?"

"Oh! Umm....maybe something outdoorsy?"

Devon cracked a grin. "Sledding?"

"On *my* toboggan, you mean?" she asked in a tone that was definitely flirty.

"That's what I was thinking."

"Will you give it to me after?"

The corners of Devon's mouth twitched. "Maybe."

"An early Christmas gift?"

Devon cocked an eyebrow. "I didn't realize we were exchanging gifts this year?"

"I don't see why not," she told him. "I'm home, aren't I?"

Yeah, and if Devon had anything to say about it, she'd be home to stay.

"Yes, you are," he answered brightly. "So, what will you get me?"

"Hmm," she said saucily. "I'll have to think on it."

Then Joy paraded up the stairs as Devon's heart soared.

Chapter Eight

JOY TIGHTLY HUGGED her sister around her neck. "*No-eeelle*! Squee!"

"Ahhh! *Jooooyyyy*! Yay!"

The two girls gripped each other firmly, bouncing up and down in the foyer of the Christmas Inn, while Gitana yapped excitedly and circled their heels.

Joy was overwhelmed with glee at seeing her twin. "It's been *soooo* long!" she squealed, caught up in their happy dance.

"I *knooowww*!"

Joy peered over Noelle's shoulder to find her dad and Gloria watching them with big happy grins.

"Can the old man get in a hug?" Walt asked them, and Noelle unwrapped herself from Joy, springing at her father.

"Hi, Dad!" she said, giving him a big hug and a kiss on his hairy cheek. Then, Noelle affectionately hugged Gloria.

"Welcome home," Gloria said sweetly.

"Where's the nugget?" Noelle asked, glancing around.

"Xavier's sleeping," Gloria answered. "But, he'll be getting up soon." She checked her watch. "In fact, it's almost time."

Noelle removed her hat and coat as Walt lifted the small suitcase she'd brought home with her. "I'll just set this in your room upstairs," he told Noelle before addressing Gloria, chuckling, "Then I'll go grab the 'nugget'!"

Gloria took Noelle's things to hang them in the downstairs coat closet and Joy took both of Noelle's hands. "It's so good to see you," she said with a contented gleam.

"Yeah." Noelle smiled tenderly. "It's been way too long."

"So, how is school?"

"Good. And, how is Italy?"

"Er..." Joy hedged. "We've got a lot to talk about."

"Yeah?"

Gloria returned to the hall on her way back to the kitchen. "Why don't you go freshen up?" she suggested to Noelle. "Then you girls can help me in the kitchen."

"Uncle David's engagement dinner is tonight," Joy said to Noelle, and Noelle's eyes danced.

"That's what I hear." Noelle looked just like Joy, but she usually wore her hair down, while Joy swept her hair up in a high ponytail. For a while, Noelle had worn glasses, but she'd gotten contacts a few years ago. The twins hugged each other again.

"Devon's coming, too," Gloria informed Noelle.

"Heard that, too!" She smiled at her loving stepmom. "Thanks, Gloria! It will be fun to see him."

"He's looking good!" Gloria said with a lilt. "Just ask Joy."

Noelle gawked at Joy when Gloria left the room. "What's that mean?" she asked in a hushed whisper.

Joy lowered her voice and spoke in impish tones. "Like I said, there's a lot to tell you."

Noelle covered her mouth in surprise. "Oh my merry Christmas! You and...?"

"No! I'm still with Giacomo."

Noelle shot her a cross look, but she was playing. "No fair hogging all the boys."

"Well, not *with* with," Joy continued in a whisper.

"What does Gloria know?" Noelle asked cagily.

Joy stole a glance at the kitchen. "I'm guessing she suspects, based on what Dad told her."

"Gee, Joy!" Noelle giggled merrily. "You've only been home a week!"

Joy eyed her uncertainly. "You're not into Devon, are you? Because if you are, Noelle, then I—"

"Who? Me?" Noelle asked with a laugh. "He's like a *brother*, Joy. We're pals, okay?"

"You're sure?"

"Sure, I'm sure." Noelle's eyes twinkled. "Besides, I'm seeing someone."

"What?"

"A super hot professor."

"*Noooo...*" Joy blinked at her. "Seriously?"

"Well, all right," Noelle said, chuckling. "He's seriously a grad student, too. But, he was my teaching assistant last semester. We flirted the whole semester through, but didn't really go out until after the class ended. Rourke didn't want things to look improper, or whatever."

"Rourke?" Joy asked, giggling. "What kind of name is that?"

"His family's background is Irish."

"Green eyes?"

Noelle giggled. "Blue."

"Dark hair or light?"

"Kind of auburn."

"Oooh! Noelle! I can't wait to meet him!"

"One step at a time, all right? Things are brand new."

"So, where have you been? What was your first date like?"

The girls trailed down the hall chattering, arm in arm, then passed Gloria working busily in the kitchen when they headed for the back staircase leading to the private family quarters upstairs. Something smelled delicious and Joy guessed Gloria was preparing those fried plantains everybody liked so much.

Gloria and Walt sometimes worked together on dinner, but mostly they took turns, with the one who wasn't cooking tending to Xavier. Joy suspected her dad was rousing Xavier from his afternoon nap in the nursery adjoining the master suite now. Joy knew Noelle would want to see Xavier before freshening up in the room that Joy and Noelle had shared since they were little. It had twin beds on antique four-poster frames and its own private bathroom.

The girls' suite was situated across a large common living area from Walt and Gloria's en suite master and the nursery. The common living area included a sitting section, outfitted like a den with a wide-screen television, and a nicely decorated Christmas tree near the rear-facing windows that looked over the snowy backyard. A small galley kitchen was positioned toward the front side of the house, and it had full-size appliances with a table for four nestled in a nook nearby.

"I'm so glad you're here!" Joy said warmly, as the girls climbed the stairs.

"I'm so happy *you're* home." Noelle's eyes sparkled sweetly as she gave Joy another hug. "Christmas wouldn't have been Christmas without you."

Chapter Nine

LATER THAT NIGHT, the Christmas family sat around the dining room table at the Christmas Inn with Devon joining them. David and Liz sat facing the low-burning fireplace, with Devon to Liz's right. The twins, Joy and Noelle, were on the other side with their backs to the hearth. Walt sat at one end of the table near the parlor, and Gloria was at the other end by the kitchen. Xavier was tucked away in bed, sleeping, and Gitana was keeping the baby company in the nursery. Two tall red candles flickered on the table and a pretty red poinsettia plant sat as the centerpiece, held in a gleaming silver planter, while snow gently fell outside the darkened windows flanking the hearth.

The group had just enjoyed a delicious Puerto Rican dinner of chicken and rice with sweet plantains on the side. Gloria had prepared a coconut flan for dessert, and everyone was raving about how delicious everything was. The plates had been cleared and Walt had just brought out a bottle of champagne.

"I believe a toast is in order," he said, filling the flutes Gloria had helped him bring to the table. "To Liz and David, and their happy news!"

"Thank y'all so much." Liz smiled, her dimples deepening. "Tonight has been so much fun."

"It has been," David agreed. "Thank you for having us over."

"You're family," Gloria said to David. Then she twinkled at Liz. "Now, you will be, too."

"I can't wait!" Liz shouted, and happy laughter broke out around the table.

Once everyone had a full glass, Walt raised his toward the newly engaged couple. "Here's to your long and happy union," he said, and the others added their cheers and *hear-hear*s.

Gloria's dark eyes sparkled. "And, to love everlasting."

People reached around each other and across the table, so everybody could clink glasses with each of the others. When Joy's glass met Devon's, a blush swept her cheeks.

"Both great things to drink to, wouldn't you say?" he asked Joy below the hubbub, and her face burned hotter.

"They are!" she said, clinking his glass with hers again. Joy took a quick sip of champagne, wondering what "love everlasting" might be like with Devon. They'd once pledged themselves to each other for eternity, a long time ago. Of course, they'd been kids then—only juniors in high school. Neither one probably really expected the magic to last.

"Jumping jelly beans!" Liz cried with alarm, setting down her glass.

Heads turned in her direction, and David laid his hand on hers. "What is it, hon? What's wrong?"

Liz's eyes were fixed on the centerpiece. "Did anybody else see that?"

Joy stared at the poinsettia and held her breath. Something had just happened to the plant, causing it to grow taller and sprout more blooms!

"Those flowers!" Liz went on, wide-eyed. "They just grew from out of nowhere!"

Walt and Gloria exchanged startled glances, and Noelle's eyebrows shot up.

"Really?" Devon asked, surprised. "I didn't—"

Suddenly, both candles snuffed out. Next, the flames in the fire were doused with a *poof*! Joy gave a shriek of surprise. And, her shriek inspired Liz to yelp louder.

"Ahh!"

"Yikes!"

Devon slowly set down his glass in the darkened dining room. "Um…is something going on?"

"Seems like we just got a…" Walt pushed back his chair and stood quickly. "Draft in the room!"

"The fireplaces in here sometimes do that," Gloria meekly explained.

"And the poinsettia?" Liz asked, still agape.

"I watered it this morning!" Gloria said.

"With Miracle-Gro!" Walt embellished.

David stared at Walt and then at his sister. But Liz just blinked and said, "Sugar plum fairy." She addressed David next. "We'll need to get some of that for our garden!"

"We're putting one in," David told the group. "At the parsonage, after we move in."

"Yeah?" Noelle asked with interest. "When will that be?"

"Sometime in May, we think," David answered.

"Or, June," Liz added. "Depends on the date for our nuptials."

David took Liz's hand. "We're still working out the details."

Walt, who'd bent toward the fireplace, already had it burning again, and Gloria had retrieved the matches to relight the candles. Joy watched the whole exchange, questioning whether she'd been responsible for the odd occurrences. Her dad had told her that other "abilities" might surface, though he hadn't been specific. But, why would growing plants have anything to do with Christmas magic? Then, Joy remembered her Uncle Ray with his incredible green thumb. He owned a Christmas tree farm and ran the North Pole Nursery. And, fire... Right! Santa needed to be able to snuff that out before traveling down chimneys. This was all incredibly zany stuff!

"Umm, Dad?" Joy said, her voice wavering. "Can I talk to you in the kitchen for a sec?"

Walt nodded in understanding. "Of course, daughter. Of course!"

***

When they were away from the others, Walt confirmed Joy's suspicions about her newly surfacing abilities. "But, I don't understand!" she said in low tones. "Why here? Why now?"

Walt's gaze darted back toward the dining room. "Those are always good questions to ask, when Christmas magic comes into play."

"Dad," Joy said a bit desperately. "I'm asking for answers."

"I'm afraid I can't give you all of those." He viewed her with compassion. "Most answers will come from you searching your heart."

"*My heart?*"

"Your heart is leading you, Joy. Toward your deepest desires."

"Gardening?" she asked, aghast, and Walt chuckled bemusedly.

"I was about to say to a certain young man."

"Making plants grow is like the mail thing, then? And, putting out fires?"

Her dad nodded sympathetically. "I didn't realize you still cared for Devon. Perhaps you didn't, either."

"Care? No, I—"

"You don't need to be afraid, sweetheart," Walt whispered warmly. "Even if it seems scary at first."

"What?" Joy asked, and her voice trembled.

"True love."

Joy considered this a moment. She thought she *was* in love—with Giacomo! Yet, none of these freaky things had ever happened around him. "But, I've known Devon forever," she said, puzzling it through.

"That may be," Walt answered. "But maybe before the timing wasn't right."

"Then, what about the cookies and milk thing in high school?" Joy asked.

Walt thoughtfully stroked his beard. "Could have been some early flare-ups. Precursors of things to come."

"Well, they're sure here now!" Joy said, growing panicked. "This thing is like a runaway train!" She studied her dad a beat longer, counting on his wisdom and his knowledge. "There must be some way to stop it."

"You're an autonomous person, of course. You can make your own choices regarding a life partner, Joy."

Joy swallowed hard, feeling totally out of sorts. "What about these weird family 'abilities'? Can I make choices about those, too?"

"Most definitely." Walt shot her a serious look. "You can go one of two ways: you can either embrace them, or deny them. If you embrace them, you can learn to control them."

"Control them? How?"

Walt's eyes sparkled reassuringly. "Practice and time."

Joy viewed Walt with trepidation. "And, if I deny them?"

Walt pursed his lips then said matter-of-factly, "Eventually, they'll go away."

"Guys!" Noelle called, entering through the breakfast area. "The others are leaving. You need to come and say goodbye."

Joy sent a petitioning look to her father.

"Things will all work out. You'll see." Walt winked encouragingly. "You're a very smart young woman, with a good head on your shoulders. You'll find your way."

Joy was glad her dad had such faith in her, but, at the moment, she felt totally lost. She'd hoped that by coming home to Christmas Town she'd be able to clear her head. Yet now, Joy felt more confused than ever.

"You okay?" Noelle whispered to her after Walt left the room.

"I think it's happening again," Joy said with a sigh.

Noelle twinkled her way. "Lots of things happened for Dad when he met Gloria."

***

Liz and David said their goodbyes, then it was Devon's turn to go. He thanked Gloria and Walt for the nice dinner, and they departed the foyer, leaving Devon with Joy and Noelle.

"Oh gosh!" Noelle said suddenly. "That's my phone!" She tugged it from her jeans pocket and stared down at its display. "Sorry, guys," she apologized to the others, "I'd better take this."

"That's funny," Joy told Devon, once Noelle had gone. "I didn't hear her phone ring, or buzz."

Devon beheld Joy warmly. "Maybe she was giving us some space."

"Devon, about earlier—"

"You mean in the dining room?"

"Yeah. Look, I know it seemed a little weird…"

"Who am I to judge?" Devon said with a shrug. "My family's different, too."

"Your folks are artists." *Not related to Santa Claus*, Joy thought, the enormity of the situation hitting her. How could she ever expect to lead a normal life? Being a distant relative of Old Saint Nick was hard enough to deal with. But, having special abilities ladled on top of that was almost too much to take. And yet, her dad had handled things perfectly fine. So had the rest of their family, according to Walt. Noelle had said she knew a little bit about their Christmas magic, but that there were certain things her dad had said she wouldn't learn until she found her true love. Was that what all of this craziness meant? Had Joy found her forever guy? In who? Giacomo? Joy tried that idea out in her mind, but it didn't exactly fit. Then she gazed into Devon's deep gray eyes.

"You were saying?" he prodded.

"Just that…" Joy licked her lips, suddenly thrown off track. "All families are different! Ha-ha! But there are levels of different! Do you know what I mean?"

Devon viewed her quizzically. "Is there something you're trying to tell me?"

"No! It's a secret!" Joy gulped, wishing she hadn't blurted out that last part.

Devon spoke with a bemused air. "I see."

"Oh, Devon..." Joy began, before stopping herself. What on earth could she say? Not the truth. Clearly. "Gosh."

"Well, whatever it is," he said kindly. "I'm sure it's not that bad."

Joy smiled tightly, trying to imagine how Devon would take it. *Oh, Santa Claus? No problem. I hear the dude is cool.* Or *Oh, yeah! I've heard of that happening before. Random DNA strains, sure.* Or *Wow, Joy. I mean, wow. Just wow! You really believe that? O-kay. I guess I'll be seeing you around!*

Devon zipped up his coat and muttered casually, "So, I've been thinking about that sledding date."

"Huh?"

"On your toboggan." His gray eyes twinkled. "How does tomorrow look for you? You want to go?"

Joy felt warm all over and her pulse pounded fiercely. "Me? Tomorrow? With you?" she asked, her head light.

"That's the general idea."

"Er...that would be...great!"

"I'll come get you around two?"

"Uh-huh."

Devon's grin lit up the room. "Super. See you then!"

Then he left, and Joy fell back against the front door, burying her face in her hands. Something was going on here with Devon. Something pretty unnerving and fantastic. And, all Joy knew was that she wanted to spend more time with him. Really, really badly. She couldn't wait for their "date," as he'd called it, at River Run, and she'd probably spend the whole night talking Noelle's ear off about it. *Wa-hooo! I'm going out with Devon!*

Joy's cheeks burned hot and her heart thumped wildly. Then she heard a *whoosh* in the parlor. Next, a *poof* sounded in the living room... Joy fretfully peered at the hearths in both places from her vantage point in the foyer.

The gas flames in both fireplaces had gone out.

Chapter Ten

THE NEXT AFTERNOON, Devon came to get Joy at a little past two in his black pickup truck. He had the toboggan tucked in its bed in back. "Hope you dressed warm enough," he said, as she climbed in the cab. "It's going to be mighty brisk up there at River Run."

Joy flashed him a bright smile. "I'll handle it."

Devon started his engine and grinned. "I'm sure you will."

As they drove down the quaint, lamppost-lined main street, Joy observed the warmly lit shops flanking the sidewalks with bright eyes. "It's so pretty here in Christmas Town," she said with a sigh. "I'd almost forgotten."

Snow dotted the landscape and dappled the windshield as they drove along, passing familiar storefronts. "It's a cool place," Devon remarked. "I've always liked it."

Joy shot him a questioning glance. "You've never thought of leaving, have you?"

"Only once."

"Yeah? Where did you want to go?"

"Italy," he said, deadpan.

"Italy?" She gave a stunned laugh. "Why?"

"I hear there are some pretty great sights there." His gaze roved over her then he set his attention back on the road. "One in particular."

From the corner of his eye, Devon saw Joy blush. "Go on!"

"I'm serious, Joy. I did think of flying to Florence."

"Oh? When?"

"When you left here seven months ago, after graduating from college." Devon shrugged. "Then I remembered you were there with Mr. Gelato, and I figured, what was the use? Three's a crowd, as they say..."

"Well, maybe you should have," she said sassily. "Should have flown to Florence."

"Yeah?" He eyed her curiously. "What would have happened then? Do you suppose the Romescos would have thrown me a party?"

"Romanos!" she said, but she was giggling. "Now, stop!"

"Are they really as rich and successful as Noelle says?"

"Actually," Joy said after a pause. "Yes."

"Must be nice."

"There are other things that matter, Devon."

"Yeah? Like what?"

"Friends," she said resolutely. "Family."

Devon was waiting for Joy to say *old boyfriends*, but naturally she didn't.

"Did you know that Noelle is seeing someone?" she asked suddenly.

"Yeah, she told me. Some Irish dude. Professor, or something."

"I'm happy for her!" Joy snuggled back against her seat. "Sounds like she likes the guy a lot."

"Then, I'm happy for her, too."

"Devon?"

"Huh?'

He could tell she was putting this gingerly. "You've always said that you and Noelle are just friends. But, did you ever...?"

"Nope." Devon turned to her as they swung through the roundabout. "Never crossed my mind."

"Funny." Joy fidgeted with the shoulder strap of her seatbelt. "That's what she says about you."

Devon chuckled reflectively. "Yeah." Devon knew this was true, because he and Noelle had talked about it early on. When they'd started hanging out, Noelle was a little uncomfortable, as she didn't want it to look like she was hooking up with her sister's ex-boyfriend. While Devon liked Noelle a lot, and obviously found her very pretty, since she looked nearly identical to Joy, he simply didn't feel that "spark" he'd experienced when he was with Joy. Noelle had told Devon not to be offended, but that she didn't feel any sparks with him, either. They'd both gotten a good laugh out of this, and things had been easy between them from there going forward.

The interesting thing about Devon's feelings for Joy was that they'd never completely gone away. Now that she was home, and it appeared he might have a chance with her, they were raging even stronger. Devon was so glad Joy was going out with him today. It seemed like forever since they'd been sledding together at River Run.

Devon turned down River Road and, before long, they were out in the countryside passing Ray and Meredith Christmas's farm.

"I haven't been to see Uncle Ray and Aunt Meredith since I've been back," Joy commented, spotting the Christmas tree farm sign. "I'll have to stop by and visit them and Kyle," she said, mentioning her cousin. Joy turned to Devon with a contented gleam. "I want to see Uncle Kurt and Aunt Savannah, too. And, their little baby, Julia. I've already seen my grandma and grandpa a couple of times."

"You have a great family," Devon said, knowing they were all very close. "I'm sure they're happy to have you home for the holidays."

Joy grinned sweetly and her smile warmed his heart. "I'm happy I'm here, too."

***

Devon settled in behind Joy on the toboggan, and her pulse thrummed. When his arms wrapped around her waist, linking in front of her, Joy's heart beat even harder. It seemed like forever since she'd been in Devon's arms. She now realized how much she'd missed his strong yet tender embrace.

"Ready?" he asked, below the winds that howled around them. Snowdrifts blew sideways at the top of the tall hill at River Run. Down below them, and far off in the distance, sat the snow-covered children's park near the riverbank. The river was mostly frozen over, with big patches of ice skirting its surface. Beyond that, wintry white mountains towered toward the blustery sky, their formidable peaks punctuated by forest-green spires where the tops of pine trees peeked through. It was a particularly cold day, even for Christmas Town, and she and Devon were the only ones out here at the moment, which only made the outing seem more intimate and special.

"Yeah," Joy answered, not entirely certain she was. Not ready for these dormant feelings that were suddenly reemerging from right out of the blue. Joy had told herself she'd moved past Devon. He'd been her first boyfriend, and a sweet one, but that phase was over, and Joy's life had moved on. Now, high on a hill at River Run, Joy couldn't help but wonder if her life was circling back around on her.

Devon leaned into her and gripped her more firmly with one arm, before pushing them off with his other hand. Then—they were off!—and zooming down the hill. Joy's heart raced and her face warmed, even as they sliced through the chilly air. Devon held her closer, with both arms now, and set his chin on her shoulder. "You all right?"

Joy nodded, but she couldn't speak. Then, all at once, her heart brimmed with happiness. They were moving at breakneck speed, and it was exhilarating. Joy hadn't done anything "fun" in so long, she couldn't recall when the last time had been. She'd worked hard to finish college, and then to start a life for herself in Italy. But, in Florence—with Giacomo—she'd never been able to completely let herself go. Giacomo was a little older, and far more serious. He was generous and kind, it was true. But, Giacomo never made Joy feel like she was flying straight up to the heavens! She shut her eyes and shouted with glee, reveling in the moment. "*Weeeeee!*"

Next, she felt Devon's embrace stiffen, in a quite unusual way. "Uh, Joy..." he murmured huskily below the wind.

She languidly laid her head back against his chest, feeling as if she were in a dream. An awesome dreamy dream! And they weren't even careening downhill anymore; it felt like they were...floating!

Joy opened her eyes with a start, to find their toboggan soaring several feet above the ground. "Yikes!" *Am I doing this? Gosh!* Soon, they'd be out over the river! Joy thought quickly, marshaling her knowledge. Santa's sleigh had reindeer. But, without animals to command, how could Joy direct the toboggan? She recalled her dad's advice: *Practice and time.* There was no time like the present, because they were approaching the kiddie park, and next the river's edge! Joy stared down at the toboggan below her and focused with all her might. *Down, toboggan! Land!*

The front of the toboggan dipped with a jerk at a downward incline, and she and Devon slipped forward. "Ooh! Ooohhh!"

"Gee, Joy!" That was Devon screaming behind her as he held on tight and leaned back to keep them from tumbling off the toboggan and into the air, as they plummeted toward a snowbank. It was an area where a huge mound of snow had collected up against the side of the life-size train engine Joy's Grandpa Buddy had built for the park.

They slammed into the snowbank with a jolt, and both got jostled on the sled. Amazingly, neither one fell off, although snow from the disturbed snowbank poured down on them, dousing their hats and coats.

"What just happened?" Devon asked, his voice thick.

Joy stared back over her shoulder and grimaced, thinking she needed a little more of that *practice*. "Er...maybe we should talk?"

Chapter Eleven

JOY WAS COMPLETELY unsure about how she was supposed to approach this. She and Devon were back at his place, where he'd offered to make them some coffee. After their chilly run-in with the snowbank, hot coffee sounded good to Joy. So did having some privacy to discuss what she needed to tell Devon.

He had a cute little apartment above Olivia Claus's shop, All Things Christmas. Olivia, a pretty redhead with green eyes in her thirties, spotted the kids when they came in the store's front door. "Oh hey, Joy!" she said sunnily. "I heard you were home for the holidays! So great to see you."

"Um, thanks!" Joy replied, her mind still preoccupied by the flying toboggan episode. "Great seeing you, too!"

Olivia cheerily eyed Devon and Joy, clearly noting they were together.

"Can I help you guys with anything?" Olivia offered sweetly. "Perhaps with picking out a gift?"

"We're not here to shop," Devon said in friendly tones. "Just headed upstairs."

"*Oh,*" Olivia said, and her green eyes twinkled.

"See you, Olivia!" Joy flushed with embarrassment as she followed Devon up the steps. Not that Joy needed to be embarrassed about anything. She and Devon had the right to be friends. And, Olivia had the right to think whatever she wanted to. ...Which was likely that Joy and Devon were looking like *more than* friends.

"Olivia gave us kind of a strange look," Devon said, as he unlocked the door to his upstairs apartment.

"She was probably wondering about the two of us being together," Joy said.

"She's seen me with other female friends." Devon shrugged and Joy experienced an unexpected twinge of jealously. "Yeah?" she asked, just as casually as she could. "Who?" She thought he would say Noelle, but he offered up the name of Noelle's friend, Pam Miller, who now waitressed at Santa's Sandwich Shop. Dark-haired, blue-eyed Pam had been Noelle's gal-pal in high school. They'd kept in touch over the years, and still got together occasionally when Noelle was in town.

"Oh, Pam!" Joy said in strained tones. "How *is* she?"

"Still doing all right." Devon glanced at Joy curiously. "Why?"

Joy smiled blandly and removed her coat. "Just wondering!"

Devon took his coat off, too, suggesting he toss their coats—along with their hats, scarves, gloves, and mittens—in the stackable dryer, which was nestled in a closet in his small but efficient single bathroom. Joy agreed, saying she'd appreciate that a lot, and offered to start the coffee.

***

Joy stared around the cheery kitchen, which had obviously been decorated by Olivia, as it held quite a few feminine touches, not typical of a bachelor pad. Joy knew that Olivia had lived in this apartment when she first came to Christmas Town, mostly because the location was so convenient, being right above her shop. When Olivia had married Nick Claus and moved into a cute little house with him on the corner of Church

Street and Mistletoe Lane, she'd rented this place out to Devon. She'd basically left it furnished, while removing her personal items, like clothing, photos, and books.

The small galley kitchen opened up on the living room with an island standing between them. The island had three tall chairs facing a dining counter on the living room side. Olivia had hand-sewn the pretty green-and-white checked seat cushions specifically to fit the chairs. The gingham-pattern cushions added a homey touch to the place and matched the curtains framing the large window at the front of the living area, which looked out on the street and at Jolly Bean Java, which was directly across the road.

The main living area housed a futon with a forest green slipcover and a couple of cranberry-colored director's chairs, and an old steamer trunk served as a coffee table. A wide-screen television sat on a console facing the futon. The lower portion of the console functioned as a bookshelf, which held volumes of carpentry books.

Joy located the coffee and filters and set the pot to brew seconds before Devon reentered the room. He smelled interestingly of fresh aftershave, and Joy wondered if he'd applied some while he was in the bathroom. The only other room in the small space was a tiny bedroom overlooking the street. Joy couldn't help but notice the double bed through the open bedroom door when they'd entered the apartment. The bed appeared to be unmade, with a comforter rumpled near its foot.

Typical of Devon, Joy reflected with a laugh. Though the rest of his apartment seemed tidy enough. She questioned whether that was because Devon had grown up a bit, or if it was more of a reflection on the fact that he didn't spend a lot of time here. He'd told her he spent nearly all his free time at his studio, including after hours when the Grand Hotel was officially closed. Woodworking was not just Devon's occupation; it was also his passion.

"Find everything okay?" he asked, stepping into the kitchen.

"Oh yeah, just fine."

Devon reached into a cabinet and pulled out two mugs, setting them on the counter. "I'm sorry if you want milk," he said apologetically. "I don't usually keep it on hand." He appeared a tad sheepish when he added, "Sugar, either."

"I don't suspect you've been baking much!" Joy said with a chuckle. She rolled her eyes, thinking of

Olivia's legendary reputation as a baker. "At least, not like Olivia."

"No." His gaze washed over her and Joy's heart thumped. Devon had always been hot in high school and college. Amazingly, he seemed even handsomer now. His features had lost some of their youthful contours and settled into the hard edges of a man's. And, his gray eyes were transformative. Joy felt like they could take her away in an instant to someplace foreign and wonderful, if she would only let them.

Joy blinked and stepped back, turning suddenly. "Should we sit while the coffee's making?" She turned to view Devon over her shoulder, and he cracked a slow, lazy grin.

"If that's what you'd like."

Joy took a seat on the futon, avoiding his eyes. Then, she took a deep breath and held it. There was no way to put this without sounding like she'd gone totally nuts.

"Joy," he said, sitting beside her. "Whatever it is, it's probably all right."

She turned to him, incredulous. "What?"

"That thing with the toboggan?" he said. "That had something to do with you being a Christmas, right?"

Joy's jaw unhinged. "But, how did you—?"

"I've been around, Joy."

"Around?" she asked weakly. "Where?"

Devon gestured toward the window. "Christmas Town." Next, he nodded firmly. "And, most importantly..." His gaze swept the floor in a telling fashion. "Living right over All Things Christmas."

"Yeah? So?" Joy asked, not following.

"So, things tend to happen sometimes. When people think nobody's watching."

"People like...Nick and Olivia?" Joy guessed.

Devon took Joy's hand and her whole body warmed. "I know, Joy."

Joy's pulse fluttered and her head spun. "Know what?"

"About Christmas magic." Devon winked, and Joy felt seriously dizzy. Reality careened around her, mixing unnervingly with what most regular individuals thought of as make-believe. Nobody truly believed in Christmas magic once its mysteries had been exposed— or did they? Gazing into Devon's eyes, Joy couldn't be sure.

"But, you can't..." she said in a whisper.

He leaned toward her and whispered back, "But, I do."

Joy pried her tongue from the roof of her mouth. "But, h...how?"

Devon squeezed her hand, and Joy was so glad he was holding it. It reminded her that she was awake and this wasn't all some ludicrous dream. Or, maybe she was dreaming?

"*Ho-ho-ho*, dear wife! How are you, Olivia?"

Nope, Joy was wide-awake! That was Nick Claus's big, booming voice from downstairs. The soundproofing in this apartment was pretty poor. *Gosh.*

"Sounds like Santa's home," Devon said, and Joy gasped.

"Nick's *not* Santa!"

"Not yet, maybe. But, he's in training."

Joy jerked back her hand. "Who told you all this, Devon?"

"Nobody had to *tell me*, Joy."

"Huh?"

"I've seen it with my own eyes."

Joy swallowed hard, trying to wrap her head around this. What exactly did Devon think he knew? What's more, how did he know it? "What do you mean, you've—?"

Devon leaned forward, setting his elbows on his knees. Then, he whispered conspiratorially. "I've been there," he said huskily. "To the N. P."

"*No.*" Joy cupped her mouth in shock. "There's no way, Devon! Nick and Olivia wouldn't have let you. If..." Joy's cheeks steamed hot. "I mean, assuming that anything you say is true."

"They not only let me," Devon replied seriously. "They asked me."

Well, so much for family secrets! Joy was completely gobsmacked. *There I believed I was dealing with news, and Devon Slade has known certain things all along!*

"What do you mean, they asked you?" she said, sitting up a little straighter. "Like invited you to an elf party, or something?"

"We don't call them elves anymore. That's not P.C."

"'We'?" *Who's "we"? What's more, how did Devon insert himself in there?* Joy blinked hard. "And, what do you mean they're not called elves anymore? What are they called, then? Reality-challenged individuals?"

Devon chuckled heartily, but Joy didn't find this the least bit funny. Somebody might have warned her at least that certain "family secrets" had been extended beyond the family. "No, not that either."

"Then, what?" Joy's voice cracked. "Little people?"

"Nick thought it stigmatizing to label them," Devon said firmly. "Unless they self-label, of course. Some do—naturally, but that is different."

Joy stared at him wide-eyed as he went on.

"Meanwhile, most prefer to be addressed by their given names, rather than get grouped into some randomly created category relating to humanlike supernatural beings with magical powers based on Germanic mythology and folklore."

Joy worked hard not to be confused by the hunk of gibberish he'd thrown at her. "So, Nick's in charge now?" she asked, attempting to stay on track.

"Not completely. We're in transition."

"Until when?"

"Maybe sometime next year."

"And, why do you keep saying 'we,' Devon?" Joy arched her eyebrows and stared at him, until he relented.

Finally, Devon blew out a hard breath. "Okay, listen," he said. "I'm not really in that deep. It's just that I've been called in once or twice in emergencies.

Production disasters and things of the like... I'm skilled at woodworking, good with my hands. Pretty handy with debugging and coding electronics, too."

Joy's gaze dropped to Devon's closed laptop, which sat on the steamer trunk in front of them.

"So..." Joy began slowly. "You've been brought in to pinch-hit?"

"Only a time or two."

"Why you?"

"Because I was here," Devon answered reasonably. "And, available. I also know Christmas Town, and a lot of its families. I always suspected, Joy. Guessed there was something going on beyond this place, that was bigger than this place—yet tied to it... Then, after Olivia rented me this apartment, I started seeing things, and, um..."

"Where's my reindeer team?" That was Nick's voice downstairs.

"They're in the yard, dear!" Olivia informed him loudly. "Waiting to be fed at home!"

"...hearing things, too," Devon confided hoarsely. "The walls *are* pretty thin."

"Well, let's lock up shop and get on *ho-ho-home*, then!" That was Nick.

"I can't wait to let you sample the new cookies I made you!" And, Olivia!

The downstairs door slammed shut, and Joy gawked at Devon. "And, I thought what I had to say would come as a surprise."

Devon observed her warmly. "You must have inherited some of it, huh? Some Christmas magic...? Nick said your family and his share common ties." He paused and then his eyes lit up. "Is that what was going on out at River Run?"

When Joy nodded numbly, Devon pressed ahead. "What else can you do?"

"Just a couple of things," Joy said with a squeak. "They're really pretty minor, compared to the flying."

Devon appeared to think on this. "The poinsettia?"

"Yep. That was me."

"And, the candles going out?"

"That, too."

"Not the mail floating through the—?"

"Yes, Devon! Oh, yes!" she cried with a whimper. "I'm really so, so sorry."

His brow creased with concern. "What are you sorry about?"

She worriedly scanned his eyes, wondering what he must think of her. "That things have gotten so out of control."

"You probably couldn't help it."

"No! I mean, yeah! I guess...I could have stopped if I wanted to. Could still..."

She drew in a shaky breath and Devon caressed her cheek with his hand.

"Joy," he asked tenderly. "What's going on?"

Her lips trembled when she murmured, "My dad says it's *trrr-uvvv...*"

"I'm sorry?" Devon's brow shot up. "What's 'truv'?"

Heat welled in Joy's eyes and she felt ridiculous. And, also really raw on the inside, like she was baring the most vulnerable and tender part of her heart. "*True love*, Devon! Gosh! Do I have to spell it out for you?"

His face broke out in a sunny grin. "True love?" he asked, clearly astounded. Devon leaned back against the futon and thought about that a moment. "Wow." Then, he brought both hands to his head and ran them simultaneously through his short choppy hair, which still looked sexy, even at this more conventional length. "Wow," he said again. And, one more time... "*Wow.*"

"Can you stop saying that, *puh-leeze*?" Joy asked, growing irritated. She'd just worn her whole heart on her sleeve, and all Devon could say was, *wow*?

He stared at her blankly and dropped his hands to his knees. "'Wow,' you mean?"

Joy gritted her teeth and yelped at him. "*Devon!*"

He jumped in his seat, before turning toward her.

"Joy," he said happily. "This is really great news."

Oh, all fine and dandy. Really great for him. What about her? Left hanging there in the breeze, like a pair of old lady's underwear stretched out on a clothesline to dry. In winter, hey! In the snow. Yeah, that. Freezing. Cold. Snow.

Devon read her cloudy expression. "Oh, Joy." He tried to take her hand again, but she pulled hers away. "Don't be mad."

"I'm not mad," she said sarcastically. "I'm feeling really hunky-dory right now, because I just said something about 'true love' and you just said—"

"'Wow'?" Devon roared with laughter, and she wanted to smack him. Really, really hard. But, that was so un-Christmas-like, and violence was definitely not encouraged in her family. Then again, Joy thought cagily, Devon wasn't precisely in her family.

"I don't like that look in your eye," he told her.

"What look?" she challenged stonily.

"The one like you used to get when we were in high school, and you were ready to throw stuff at me."

"I never threw stuff at you, Devon."

"No. But, sometimes—come on, admit it—you wanted to."

"Okay. All right. I wanted to!"

"Joy? What is—?"

"Devonnnn!" she growled and grabbed his arms. "How dare you! How dare you do this to me!"

"*Wha-at* did I do?" he asked, stumbling over his words, as she pinched into his biceps.

"You just...just..." Gosh, his muscles were rock-hard! When did that happen? Devon hadn't been this built when they'd dated before. *Must be all the working out. Or woodworking. Whatever*, Joy mused, her pulse fluttering.

Joy tried not to think about his arms, or his chest—which actually appeared pretty solid, too. And, those shoulders that seemed to have broadened more than just a bit. And, those smoldering gray eyes that were sizzling wicked-hot, and making her lose all sense of reason at the moment.

"You really do like me, don't you?" Devon asked with an amazed grin.

"I...I never said that," Joy muttered, feeling a little breathy.

"Well, I'm hoping it's true." Devon leaned toward her, and Joy felt the room spin. Or maybe the earth was tumbling over itself, whirling her upside down, then setting her right again. "Joy," he said softly, cupping her cheek. "Haven't you guessed?"

She waited as he moved closer, then her hands shifted to his shoulders. She needed to grip them to keep herself from falling up against him...and collapsing into his embrace. Oh, but how she wanted Devon to hold her. So badly.

"It's not just you." Devon gently stroked her cheek. "I'm still hung up on you, too. That's why I said 'wow,' Joy. I was so happily amazed. Incredibly pleased and stunned to think...to hope..." Devon took her in his arms and his voice grew thick. "That you could still care for me." He viewed her longingly. Wistfully. "Do you?"

Emotion welled within her and tears leaked from her eyes. Joy's analogy to her father earlier had been apt. And, there *was* no stopping this runaway train. Was this really *true love*, in all its infuriating yet incredibly awesome iterations? "Yes, Devon," she said as steadily as she could manage. "I do."

He smiled tenderly then and drew nearer. "That's so great to hear."

Devon's lips brushed over hers, and Joy felt warm winds feather across her face. Then, she heard the faraway cry of seagulls. Everything around them was airy, and wonderful, and light.

"Devon," she sighed, feeling like she'd wanted this forever, because maybe she had.

"I'm here," he answered, holding her close. Then Devon pulled Joy up against him, and took her breath away.

Chapter Twelve

THE NEXT COUPLE weeks were two of the finest weeks of Joy's life. She and Devon spent every waking moment together that they could. At his insistence, she even set up an easel in his woodworking studio and kept him company in the evenings when he was working after hours. Devon had several commissioned pieces he needed to complete before Christmas, and Joy didn't want to cause him to miss any deadlines. Then again, she couldn't bear not being with him. Devon *had* gifted Joy with the toboggan after that first day at River Run. Later, he'd hinted he had another special present in store, but that she'd have to be a good girl and wait until Christmas to receive it. Joy had laughed in return, saying she also had a surprise in progress for him.

Meanwhile, they'd gone sledding again—several times—and ice skating at Miller's Pond. Olivia had even let them take out a few horses for a snowy ride at Sleigh Bell Stables. And, everywhere Joy and Devon went...Christmas magic seemed to follow. Things just seemed to occur when they were together. But, Joy was taking the reins on those mysterious happenings. They'd only been accidently flying in the toboggan a few times since that first excursion. And, their landings were certainly getting smoother!

Joy and Devon joked that the special magic they shared might not only be due to Joy's family heritage; it might be partially on account of that Commitment Cookie they'd shared as teenagers, too. Though, naturally, neither one knew for sure. Back when Noelle had been Hannah's cookie intern, Joy had asked Noelle to procure a coveted Commitment Cookie for her from the Christmas Cookie Shop. Joy and Devon had each eaten half of it in the back alley behind the Grand Hotel, which had been closed at the time. Then, they'd giddily meandered around town, in their happy, puppy-love bubble, until they'd come to the roundabout sign that proclaimed:

Welcome to Christmas Town, Tennessee...
Where everyday dreams come true!

Joy had asked Devon if they had a future then, and he'd kissed her in reply. That had been the real start of the relationship between them. They'd moved from flirty interest in each other to officially going out, all in the course of one day—and, after ingesting that Commitment Cookie. They'd joked and laughed about it later, because eating the red-and-pink heart-shaped cookie had made them both feel kind of silly. All warm and tickly inside, and like they had to kiss, and kiss, and kiss as much as possible in those first twenty-four hours! Ha-ha!

Joy still giggled about it, remembering how big and puffy her lips had gotten. She'd had to put ice on them back at home. Then, she'd had to concoct some story for her dad and Noelle about having burned her mouth on hot cocoa. *On a hot boyfriend was more like it.*

Joy sighed audibly, thinking Devon was even hotter today. His kisses sure seemed twice as steamy, and everything about him was so breathtakingly manly. He was a grown-up now, with his own place to live and his own studio, which was so cool. Joy was very proud of Devon for sticking up for his art, and doing what he wanted to do. He'd never once gotten sidetracked. The one who'd done that, Joy saw now, was her, by moving to Italy. She felt so happy to be back in Christmas Town. And, so peaceful, like this was where she really belonged. It was also a place Joy was starting to see herself remaining for the long-term.

Since she'd been a teen, she'd always had her eye on a cute little bungalow on Mistletoe Lane. Just recently, Joy had learned from Grandpa Buddy, who was a part-time realtor, that the place was about to go up for sale. Joy had found herself strolling past the house a lot during these past few weeks, and every time she'd gazed at the cozy, one-story charmer, she'd thought of Devon. She'd even had a vision of the two of them frolicking in the snowy front yard with a couple of children. Her and Devon's kids... And, this time, the images hadn't been fuzzy. They'd come out crystal clear.

Joy had stopped into Jolly Bean Java to pick up coffee for her and Devon, and she planned to carry it back to the Grand Hotel. Devon was working late tonight, and she was keeping him company. Afterward, they planned to go out for a late dinner of yummy pizza at the Reindeer Pub. Joy had just retrieved two steaming paper cups from Mr. Smith, the barista, after paying him, and was on her way out the door. That's when she saw Giacomo Romano enter the café, and both cups slipped from her hands.

Chapter Thirteen

COFFEE SPLATTERED AT Joy's feet and customers seated nearby scooted back their chairs. A couple of helpful coffee shop patrons rushed to assist her, by scurrying over with napkins and dumping them on the spreading pools of coffee that were approaching Joy's lime green snow boots. But, all she could say was, "Giacomo," her gaze fixed on the great-looking Italian.

"*Cara!*" he said fretfully. "Are you okay?" Giacomo dashed toward her, and Joy stepped back, nearly skidding on a slick spot on the floor.

"Wha—what are you doing here?" This was crazy! Nuts! Giacomo was supposed to be in the Italian Alps skiing with his family.

"I had to see you. Joy, please." His handsome face hung in a frown, and Joy had never seen him looking so downtrodden. "Can we talk?"

"You flew all the way here from Italy just to—?"

"Talk, yes. I promise." He held up both hands. "I needed to see you in person. Even if you send me away."

This was so unlike him. Giacomo appeared so wounded. So contrite...

"I thought we were taking a break?" But, even as she said it, her voice warbled.

"A break, I know." His dark eyes glistened. "Maybe a bad idea."

"No," Joy said in a rush. "Maybe it was a good one. Giacomo." She glanced around at the interested folks who were watching them. "I have some things to tell you. But, not here."

He nodded then bent to help Joy clean up her mess. Caleb Smith stepped around the counter with a mop and pail, and Joy apologized to him profusely.

"It's all right, hon," he said in a fatherly fashion. "Why don't you and your friend run along." Joy didn't know whether she'd imagined it, but it almost seemed like Mr. Smith had sent Giacomo a steely look. "I'll clean up here."

Joy stepped outside feeling stunned, like she'd just been broadsided by a two-by-four.

"Where shall we go to talk?" Giacomo queried softly. "The Christmas Inn?"

"Yeah," Joy said. "Home would be good." She tugged her cell from her coat pocket, intending to phone Devon. "But, I've got to make a call first."

***

Back at the Christmas Inn, Gloria greeted them wide-eyed, when she spotted Joy and Giacomo in the front hall. "Well, *hel-lo...*?" she said perplexedly. She turned to Giacomo and her forehead rose. "Giacomo?"

Gitana bounded into the foyer, yapping excitedly. But, when Giacomo reached out a hand to greet her, the dog withdrew with a wary gaze. Gloria shot a look at Gitana and then at Giacomo. "Well, where are my manners?" she said, snapping to. "Merry Christmas, Giacomo. This is a surprise."

"Yes, well, I'm sorry," he said deferentially. "But, don't worry. I'm not staying." He cast a mournful gaze at Joy. "Unless Joy wants me to."

"I think we need a minute," Joy told Gloria.

"Of course." Gloria nodded. "Make yourselves comfortable in the living room." She forced a pleasant grin. "Can I get either of you anything?"

Both declined and Gloria exited the living room through the library. She caught Walt on the threshold and gently pushed him back.

"What?" he asked gruffly. "What's *he* doing here?"

"Sweetheart," Gloria said calmly, pushing a little harder against Walt's chest and forcing him to back up. "I think we need to let them talk."

Walt harrumphed, but Gloria tugged him away, whispering in low tones, until Joy heard their footsteps retreating toward the kitchen.

Giacomo sat beside Joy on the sofa and shifted uncomfortably. His reddened eyes brimmed with worry. "I want to apologize."

"Giacomo—"

"No, please," he said gently. "I really need to tell you."

"Tell me?"

"About how wrong I was." Giacomo shared an earnest look. "I should have been more understanding about your family, Joy. Shouldn't have made you choose—"

"But, you said—"

"I know, but I was wrong." He tried to take her hand but Joy scooted away a little further on the sofa. "The Romanos are not like the Christmases," he told her. "Not like your family. I was here with you in Christmas Town last year, and I know what the holiday is like for everyone here. A very big deal." He gave a wan smile. "And for us?" Giacomo shrugged. "It's just another opportunity for a vacation. A vacation that might be taken at any other time of year."

"But, you wanted me to meet your sister—"

"Margherita would be happy to see you at any other time. The holidays make her a bit cranky, anyway."

"Cranky?"

"Her kids are always complaining. What they have is never enough. It seems they always want more."

"I'm sorry," Joy said sympathetically. "What about Margherita's husband?"

"Holidays make him cranky, too," Giacomo said, and both of them laughed.

Joy was grateful for the brief lighthearted reprieve in the midst of all this heaviness. She needed to tell Giacomo about Devon, and about how she'd decided her life was in Christmas Town. She'd had so many signs, after all, that Devon was the one.

"Giacomo," Joy began tentatively. "I...have something to tell you. Actually, I think it was good that we took a break, because—"

"Because I was being a heel!" Giacomo broke in. "An idiot! We had wonderful times in Florence." He met her eyes, and, in spite of herself, Joy admitted it was true. She and Giacomo had enjoyed incredible times in Italy, many of them extremely romantic.

Giacomo was demonstrative and had a flourish for doing unexpected things like flying her to Venice for dinner, then letting her know their surprise picnic would be in a gondola he'd reserved for them at sunset. Joy sighed heavily, finding herself reluctantly getting swept away on the rushing tide of memories. Giacomo was not a bad kisser, either. Truth was, he was really good at it... In that experienced, European way that probably meant he'd already kissed dozens of other women. Though, what should that matter to Joy when he'd committed only to her?

But, I'm not committed to Giacomo! Joy gave herself a swift mental kick. *It's Devon. Devon that I...* Joy's mental wheels stopped turning as she stared down at the ring box in Giacomo's hand. He'd pulled it from his jacket pocket and flipped it open, revealing the most enormous solitaire diamond Joy had ever seen in her life.

"I know I've been stupid about this," Giacomo began. "But, as you Americans say, I've finally wised up. Joy..." He reached for her hand, and—this time—Joy was so stunned she let him take it. "You are the love of my life. I've known many, many women, but none have even come close to you. We tried transcontinental and that was tough. We tried having you in Italy." He watched sadly as a tear slid down her cheek. "And, that apparently failed. Now, I know why, *cara*." He squeezed her hand. "It's because your heart is here, right here in Christmas Town, and taking you out of Tennessee is like ripping your heart from your body." His eyes glimmered, taking on a glossy sheen. "I love you far too much to do that. That's why I've decided that—if you'll marry me..." Giacomo swallowed hard. "I'll move with you to Christmas Town."

"What?" Joy asked, completely floored.

"After I finish my studies," he said. "I spoke to an architect in town today, and he said he might be needing my services. He's overwhelmed with projects and has other obligations abroad."

"Nick?" Joy asked unsteadily. "You talked to Nick Claus?"

Giacomo nodded then continued, "If that doesn't work out, I'll search for other opportunities in the neighboring towns."

"You'd really do that?" Joy asked, still in a state of disbelief. "You'd really do that for me?"

"Joy." Giacomo's dark eyes glimmered. "I'd do anything for you."

Then, he pried the exquisite ring from its satiny cushion and Joy gasped.

Next, the fireplace in the living room went out, and Joy gasped louder.

"Walt!" Gloria called from the dining room. "The fireplace just went out in here!"

"Well, I'll be darned," Walt said, hollering back from the neighboring room. "The one in the library, too!"

Joy stared with trepidation into the parlor, seeing the flames in that gas hearth had abruptly been extinguished, as well. "I have to think!" she said, leaping to her feet.

"Think?" Giacomo stared up at her, the ring still poised in his hand. He appeared so crushed. Really, really let down. Joy thought of how she'd felt when she'd spilled her guts to Devon, and Devon hadn't reacted right away—other than to say, wow. Joy was now leaving poor Giacomo in the same excruciating limbo.

"Giacomo," she began quietly. "I'm so, so sorry, but..."

Earnest brown eyes peered into her soul and Joy felt her heart ping. Giacomo was willing to move here—for her. Completely change his life. Devon had never changed anything about his. He'd been single-minded in his purpose to stay in Tennessee, and had been willing to let Joy go off to Italy, without saying so much as a word. Even when he still had feelings for her and believed that she was making a mistake.

Well, perhaps Joy had been the one making the mistake now, thinking that she was fated to be with Devon because of some silly cookie they'd shared six whole years ago! *Look at this man. Look at his face.* Giacomo's whole heart was breaking apart, and Joy was the cause of it. Did she really want to say no, and send him away forever? After all the courage it had taken him to come here, and given the sacrifices he was willing to make? Would Giacomo still feel the same way about her, when Joy shared about Christmas magic? Somehow, Joy imagined he would. What else could explain every single fireplace in the Christmas Inn going out at once? Maybe Joy didn't have *one* special someone...perhaps she had *two*? And now that the timing was right, she had to make a choice.

Joy sank back down onto the sofa in a daze, considering the Romanos and how they might take Giacomo's move. "What about your family?"

"They completely understand." He grinned handsomely and his smile warmed Joy's heart. "We Italians are all about love."

Chapter Fourteen

DEVON PROWLED AROUND his studio, feeling restless
and agitated. He'd tried to focus on a few tasks, but
he'd been unable to. Devon was not happy to get Joy's
call saying she was canceling their date. He was even
less pleased to learn it was because *Gelato Romesco*
had come to town. What unbelievably bad luck. Right
when things had been going so great between him and
Joy, too. Devon had run into Noelle later at the Merry
Market and learned that Giacomo was staying that
night at the Christmas Inn, before returning the next
day to Italy. At least that was something. The guy was
leaving. But, why had he come here to begin with? To
try to woo back Joy, obviously.

Devon had tried to casually ask Noelle about the
details, but Noelle had been unusually tight-lipped,

saying maybe it was best if Devon spoke directly to Joy. Which would have been a fine idea, if Joy had been answering her phone and not letting calls go straight to voice mail. She hadn't been on social media, either, so Devon had no way to know what Joy was thinking. Or, maybe more importantly, who she was thinking about.

Could Joy honestly be considering getting back together with the Italian dude? After the way he'd made her choose about her family, and the holidays? Devon would never do that. Then again, Devon never would have to, since both his family and Joy's lived here. Devon was crazy with worry and raw fear clenched in his belly. Joy couldn't...wouldn't. Not after these past few weeks. Not given what Devon knew, about her Christmas magic, and the Christmas and Claus families. Devon was on the inside now, accepted into their secretive circle. Joy would never go outside that and take a stranger like Giacomo into her confidence. No matter how wealthy or attractive he was.

Tomorrow was Christmas Eve and Devon was scheduled to take Joy to the Christmas Town Ball. Noelle had graciously backed out, saying she didn't feel right going now that she was seeing Rourke, anyway. But, Devon understood Noelle was just being kind. She knew that Devon and Joy were seeing each other again, and wanted them to attend the special gala together. Joy had already shopped for a dress at the Merry and Bright Boutique, and had showed it off by doing a little fashion show in the store for Devon. Joy looked fantastic in the emerald green gown, but now Devon fretted over whether or not she was going to wear it. Was Joy even going to the ball, still? Or, would she be changing her mind about that and flying back to Italy?

It would help if she answered her phone. Instead of that, Joy suddenly appeared in the doorway to Devon's studio.

"Joy!" Devon said in surprise. "How did you get in?"

"I saw Liz Martin downstairs," she explained, looking meek. "Liz let me in when she was leaving."

He studied her worried expression and fear knotted his gut. "Is everything okay?"

She eyed the floor a moment before looking up. "I guess you heard that Giacomo was here?"

Only from everybody in town, Devon thought with an inner grumble.

"But, he's gone now?"

Joy nodded. "He left this morning."

Devon felt awash with relief before he caught the glimmer of tears in Joy's eyes. "And?"

"He's asked me to marry him, Devon."

Devon felt like someone had pulled the rug out from under him. "Of course you said no, right?"

Her failure to answer was like a sucker punch to Devon's chest. "Wait..." He eyed her disbelievingly. "You didn't?"

Joy set her jaw and avoided Devon's gaze. "I told him I'd think about it."

"Think about what, Joy?" Devon hated the fact that his voice rose shrilly. "You don't love the guy, you said so. You told me you cared about m...?" An arrow shot through Devon's heart at Joy's distant look, and that arrow was flaming hot—scorching through the whole of him. Devon had to steel himself to keep from staggering. "This is unbelievable," he said at last.

"I'm sorry," she said. "It's confusing."

"Confusing?" Devon asked, growing panicky. No way could this happen. He wasn't going to lose Joy to what's-his-name-he-couldn't-even-pronounce—again. "What's so confusing? You couldn't stand being away from Christmas Town and your family. Now you're ready to chuck everything, and what?" Devon steadied his voice to keep it from rising further. "Move to Italy?"

"Actually, no," Joy said without looking happy about it. She truthfully appeared kind of lost. "Giacomo said he's willing to move here."

"To Christmas Town?" Devon asked, and this time his voice cracked apart like a teenager's. "Wow." The blood drained from Devon's face when he saw his worst nightmares coming true. He wouldn't just be losing Joy to Giacomo. He'd get the chance to see the happy pair in and around Christmas Town, day after painstaking day. And here Devon had believed Joy to be loving and fun. Even after she'd let him down the first time, he'd trusted her enough to open back up his heart. Now she was going to smash it to pieces all over again. She might as well have used a wrecking ball.

"So, these past few weeks in Christmas Town?" Devon asked hoarsely. "All the time we spent together...that meant nothing?"

Joy's chin warbled as she stood on the threshold. "I never said that."

Devon stared at Joy in shock, and then said, "I guess you didn't have to."

"If you'll just give me some time—"

"More time?" He laughed bitterly. "And, then what? I pass you the knife so you can twist it in deeper?"

"Devon—" She sighed and wiped her cheek, which was damp. "Please."

"You have a whole lot of nerve, you know that?" he said, refusing to walk toward her. At the moment, Devon felt like keeping his distance. He probably should have done that all along. "Coming here and asking for 'time.' Telling me that Romesco guy—"

"Romano," she corrected with a sniff.

"Joy!" he said sharply. "Look at me." When she did, wide-eyed, Devon continued stonily. "I. Don't. Care."

"About...?"

"Any of it," Devon said dismissively. "You go ahead and marry your Romeo. From where I sit, the two of you were made for each other."

Joy inhaled sharply and her shoulders shook, as she quietly sobbed. "I didn't want it to go like this."

"Then you must not have thought this out, Joy. Because I did. You know that? A very long time ago. I decided that you were the girl for me, and then you left me."

"That's not fair! You told me to go!"

"Because it was better for you. I didn't want to hold you back." Devon pursed his lips stoically and then added, "And, perhaps this guy is better for you, too. I mean, what other guy would move clear across the Atlantic?"

"I guess not you, huh?" Joy said, her tears running more freely.

"I guess not me," he said evenly.

Joy choked back a sob and turned on her heel. "I'm leaving for Florence the day after Christmas. Giacomo wants me to meet the rest of his family."

"Well, that's just great!" Devon called after her. "I hope you have a really nice flight!"

Joy tore down the stairs, taking them two at a time until she reached the enormous foyer. Devon chased after her and shouted angrily from the landing, "I guess you won't be wanting your Christmas present!"

"I guess you won't be wanting yours!" she screamed back.

Devon fumed and stared down at her. "What about the ball?"

"Take Noelle!" she shouted, without turning. Then Joy yanked open the Grand Hotel's heavy front door, and shut it behind her with a *bang*.

Chapter Fifteen

"I REALLY WISH you'd go to the ball, Noelle."

Noelle passed Joy another tissue, as they sat on one of their matching twin beds together. They were in the private family quarters section of the Christmas Inn, and their dad and Gloria were downstairs fixing an early dinner.

"I can't," Noelle said. "I already told Gloria and Dad I'm babysitting."

"I'll babysit."

"You're not fit to babysit," Noelle said, giving Joy's shoulder a hug. "I'll stay here to help you."

Joy nodded gratefully, because the truth was she didn't totally trust herself to be really good company for Xavier. Though she certainly would be competent at caretaking; it was far less likely that Joy could be cheery.

"You still want to go to church with us at five?" Noelle asked her.

"Yeah," Joy said. "I always like that service, and I'll want to see Uncle David."

"Then after, we'll come back here and play with Xavier before bathing the little cutie and putting him to bed. And, then..." Noelle leaned into Joy, and said merrily, "Girls' night! How does popcorn and a chick flick sound?"

Joy smiled, heartened. "Sounds like I've got a pretty great sister."

"You've got that part right," Noelle said, giving Joy's shoulder a squeeze.

Joy wearily viewed Noelle. "Do you think I'm doing the right thing?"

"In going to Italy? Sure. Giacomo wants you to meet the rest of his family, before you make your decision, and that seems only fair. The guy did make it a point to meet all of us."

"Yeah."

"I can't believe Giacomo's actually willing to move to Christmas Town!" Noelle said, her big blue eyes wide. "That's dedication right there."

"I know," Joy said, still marveling at Giacomo's decision. "It surprised me, too."

"Not just any guy would do that, you know," Noelle said cajolingly.

Joy smiled in sad reflection. "I know."

***

Devon didn't know how he was going to get through this Christmas, but he supposed he'd do it like he had all the other ones before. Glumly. Only, this time would be worse, because having Joy home—and her giving him hope—had been like reopening an old wound. While he hadn't been super happy without Joy in his life, Devon had carved out an existence he'd found satisfying. He had friends and coworkers he liked spending time with, a cool place to live, and a job that he loved. Devon had dated a few people casually, but he'd never felt that same spark he'd experienced with Joy. Then, she'd come home for the holidays, and Devon had dared to hope for a new beginning. What a huge letdown that had been. And now, tonight, instead of going to the annual Christmas Town Ball with either of the Christmas twins, Devon was sitting at his parents' house with his little sister, Annabel, watching reruns of hokey old Christmas movies on TV, while both their parents were partying at the Grand Hotel.

Annabel was in the eighth grade, so too young for the ball, but apparently not too young to be interested in boys. Devon had a hunch that Annabel had a crush on Ray and Meredith Christmas's son, Kyle, who was a few years older, because she kept coming up with excuses for running into him lately. Kyle worked at his parents' nursery on Santa Claus Lane, and Annabel had repeatedly run down there for various things she was sure her parents wanted for their shop and their home. She'd even procured a sprig of mistletoe for Devon to hang above the doorway to his studio.

Not that he'd done that, since that didn't seem professional. Now, Devon was extra glad he hadn't. Since his last memory of that doorway came with Joy standing in it, appearing all brokenhearted. It probably *was* heartbreaking letting the same guy down. *Two times in a row*, Devon thought with a tense scowl.

His cell buzzed and he saw it was Noelle, saying she was sorry about the ball, and that they would catch up sometime. Devon thought of the writing desk he'd made Noelle, but didn't suspect that tomorrow would be the best time to drop by the Christmas Inn. Joy clearly wouldn't want to see him. And, maybe Noelle wouldn't want to, either. Devon hoped his falling-out with Joy wouldn't color his friendship with Noelle, though he understood that it might. In which case, Devon would have lost doubly this season.

He tried to focus on the TV movie, but his thoughts kept reeling back to that other gift he had purchased. The one he'd picked out especially for Joy in the next town over, where Devon's friend Pam said there was a really good jewelry shop. He'd been impulsively stupid to buy it. Devon saw that especially now. And, in any case, Romeo had gotten there first. There was no competing with *his* proposal, Devon was sure. Nor with the Italian guy's money, charisma, or charm, it seemed. It was a good thing Devon hadn't formally paid for and picked up his purchase. The jeweler had it on hold, and Devon was planning to call and cancel his order. If he lost his deposit, so be it. Things probably couldn't get any worse for him this Christmas anyway.

Devon slunk down on the sofa beside Annabel, and dug his hand into the bowl of popcorn they shared between them.

"It's fun having you home on Christmas Eve," she said sweetly. Devon knew that Annabel looked up to him, and she was a sweet kid, with big gray eyes like his and long black hair, parted in the middle.

"Thanks, kiddo!" Devon affectionately tussled her hair then spoke from the heart. When the rest of the world let him down, at least he had his family. "I'm really glad to be here, too."

***

Christmas Day at the Christmas Inn went off well enough, with everyone gratefully admiring the presents they'd received from one another. Walt and Gloria were especially pleased by the beautiful painting Joy had made them of Fiesole, and made a big show of mounting it immediately over the mantel in the library, letting it take the place of the previous winter landscape scene that had hung there. Without question, though, baby Xavier was the star of the show, excitedly enjoying his new hobby-horse-design bouncy chair, which he rode up and down, and up and down—until he finally became as exhausted as the adults had become just by watching him, and had to be laid down for his nap.

"Jumping jelly beans, that kid is a spitfire," Liz said cheerfully from beside David on the sofa. They all sat around the hearth in the library, with Joy also on the sofa and Gloria and Walt in the wing chairs. Noelle sat on the floor beside Gitana, rubbing the lazy hound's belly. Gloria and Walt had prepared a delicious Christmas dinner, with Joy and Noelle's help, then Liz and David had taken over cleaning up the kitchen afterwards. Now, they all rested contentedly around the fire, reflecting on the blessings of the day and the season.

"It's so nice that you're home this year," Liz said to Joy, clearly not knowing about the drama that had gone on since Joy's return. Liz sweetly took Uncle David's hand and grinned at Joy. "I hope you'll be able to make it home for our wedding?"

"She's moving home!" Walt said authoritatively.

When David's brow rose, Gloria further added, "For good." She turned to her stepdaughter. "Isn't that right, honey?"

"Yep! That's the plan." Color warmed Joy's cheeks. "I'm just going back to Italy for a few weeks first."

"To pick up your things?" Liz asked Joy, after she and David shared a look. Clearly, both were too polite to ask about Giacomo, but they must have supposed Joy and he had experienced some kind of falling-out.

"To meet the rest of Giacomo's family." Joy tried to inject a note of enthusiasm into her voice. "He's asked me to marry him."

"*Sugar plum fairy.*" Liz's eyes grew wide. Then, she quizzically studied Joy's dour expression. "You are happy about this, sweetie?"

Joy gave a tremulous smile. "Ecstatic, sure!" She put on a brave face and chattered effusively about Giacomo and what a great guy he was, taking care to note that she hadn't totally decided to accept his wedding proposal. There was so much to work out still, and they both had tons of time.

Noelle took a cue from her sister, and helpfully changed the subject, suggesting they all play a family game around the fire in a little bit. This comment seemed to jog something in Gloria's memory, and she turned toward her husband.

"Walt, before I forget to tell you," Gloria began as an aside, "the Hearth and Home guy said it was what you expected: an air bubble in the gas line."

"What Hearth and Home guy?" Joy queried, feeling like she'd missed something. She hadn't noticed any repair people coming around.

"Yesterday while you were in town," Gloria answered, "a repairman stopped by to look at the fireplaces."

"Oh?" Joy asked with alarm.

"It was some fluke thing." Walt caught himself suddenly and stared straight at Joy. "Wait a minute... You didn't think...? When Giacomo was here...?"

Joy felt herself pale. Then, reality hit hard and she realized it scarcely mattered. So what if she'd misread that sign about the fires going out, and there was no Christmas magic with Giacomo? The special connection she'd shared with Devon hardly seemed significant anymore, anyway. Devon hadn't been any more willing to fight for Joy now than he had been two and a half years ago, when she'd first gone to Florence. While she didn't believe he should have stopped her from having the once-in-a-lifetime experience of studying abroad, if Devon had still loved her and had wanted to make their relationship work, he should have mustered the courage to tell Joy so. Then again, Joy realized sadly, she hadn't fought to save their relationship, either.

At this point, though, depressing reflections on things that "might have been" seemed pointless. If Joy's emotional ties to Devon hadn't been severed completely two and a half years ago, they were clearly cut now. He'd appeared mighty ticked off at Joy when they'd parted a few days ago at his studio. And, the truth was she couldn't totally blame him. Although, honestly? Devon's words and actions had hurt Joy badly, too.

She and Devon stood at an impasse, Joy guessed. And, Joy didn't want the sort of guy who pulled up his drawbridge and shut himself off at the first sign of trouble. She needed a mature man, one who could admit his faults and welcome her with open arms. Joy understood now that man was Giacomo Romano. Giacomo was willing to build a life with her in Christmas Town, and Gloria and her dad seemed mighty happy about that. Okay, maybe Walt was *resignedly happy*. But he'd said he would definitely support the marriage, if Joy decided that's what she wanted. Any fellow who loved his daughter enough to pull up stakes and move clear across the Atlantic was clearly worth his salt.

Walt stood and walked toward the bar, grabbing a bourbon bottle. "Shall we all have a little eggnog and toast to your engagement?"

Joy startled until she realized her dad was speaking to David and Liz. Joy definitely hadn't decided on her future yet. Or, had she?

"Sure!" David said merrily.

"Sounds good," Liz agreed with a dimpled grin.

Noelle sent Joy a sisterly look and gave a play pout. Noelle always knew what Joy was thinking, and today her intuition was spot on. Joy was thinking she was going to marry Giacomo, because he'd been the one to man up and ask her. Only, way down deep in her heart, Joy was secretly wishing it had been Devon who'd taken the chance.

Chapter Sixteen

DEVON WENT INTO work early on the morning of December 26 and he stayed there all day. The Grand Hotel was fairly quiet, with just a handful of shoppers browsing the artists' studios. With everybody's Christmas shopping done, most folks simply wanted a place to get out and stretch their legs, while staying protected from the elements. It was snowing hard, but that hadn't stopped Joy's flight from taking off in Knoxville. Against Devon's better judgment, he'd checked the airline schedule on his phone.

He'd had a reasonably decent Christmas with his folks, and his mom had made great food. At the last minute on Christmas Eve, Devon had asked Annabel if she felt like going to the eleven o'clock Christmas service, and she'd been very excited about doing something so grown-up. Devon wasn't sure he wanted to go. He normally wasn't big into church, or anything. But he did like the holiday hymns and was feeling kind of lonely, even in Annabel's company.

Joy's Uncle David had done a great job with the service, and being among Christmas Town's parishioners had made Devon remember a lot of things. Like him and Joy going to the late-night service together, while joking about what Santa would bring them each, depending on whether they'd been naughty or nice. Devon and Joy had a habit of swapping Christmas gifts afterwards, back at the Christmas Inn in the library. Devon liked that room. It was cozy. He could see why Joy's family spent so much of their time there.

Devon had never been able to stay more than a few minutes past midnight, because Joy's strict dad, Walt, wouldn't allow it. But, he'd been there to wish Joy a merry Christmas, before the two of them spent the remainder of the holiday with their respective families. Sitting in that pew in the Corner Church, Devon had realized how much he missed being around Joy at Christmastime. Deep down in his soul, he pretty much missed her all the time. But something about Christmas made the ache of being without her feel even worse.

"Knock-knock! Hel-lo!"

Devon looked up from his table saw and pushed his goggles on top of his head. The town mayor, Lou Christmas, stood in his doorway. Lou was also Walt Christmas's mom and Joy's grandmother. Light brown hair, which was frosted at the tips, brushed the shoulders of her fake animal-print coat. She wore a red felt Santa hat on her head and was in the process of removing her gloves.

"Mrs. Christmas," Devon said with surprise. "Hey. How are you doing?"

"Just fine, Devon. And you?" She gave a thin smile and small laugh lines formed around her eyes as she tucked her gloves in her pockets.

"I'm good," Devon said, making an effort to be conversational. He had no clue why Lou was here, but wondered if it might have to do with his studio, since Lou oversaw the Grand Hotel Committee. "I hope you had a nice Christmas with your family."

"I did! And, you?"

"Very nice, thanks."

Lou strolled into his studio and glanced around, noting the writing desk shoved against a wall. "That's a lovely piece," she said, eyeing it.

"I made it for Noelle."

Lou's brow rose at this. "Oh?

"I'd planned to give it to her for Christmas." Devon removed his goggles and set them on his workbench. "Only, I..." He struggled with how to put it. "I haven't had time to deliver it."

"Hmm, I see." Lou walked over to the desk and ran her palm across the polished surface. "It's gorgeous, Devon." She looked up and pinned him with her gaze. "What a very nice gift."

Devon suddenly had the notion that Lou wasn't here to talk about his studio. Her mission was much more personal.

Lou cocked her chin and studied him. "Joy left for Italy today."

"That's what I..." A lump formed in Devon's throat and he coughed into his hand to clear it. "...hear."

Lou's perfectly manicured eyebrows shot up. "Well. What do you intend to do about it?"

Devon stared at her, flummoxed. "Do?"

Lou crossed her arms in front of her. "Devon Slade," she said tersely. "Don't pretend that you don't love my granddaughter, because I know you do."

"Mrs. Christmas—"

"I have eyes, you know," she barreled ahead like a steamroller. "Some even accuse me of having them in the back of my head, because nothing escapes my notice in Christmas Town." She paused and drew in a breath. "The moment Joy returned for the holidays, the two of you got together, and you were practically inseparable until the Italian came back to get her."

"His name is…Giacomo," Devon said, finally getting it right. "Romano."

"Yes, yes." Lou waved her hand. "And, he's a very nice fellow, too. Don't think that I don't believe that. Joy has very good taste. She wouldn't have taken up with Giacomo if he were otherwise. But, here's the thing, young man," Lou said, striding toward him as Devon watched her wide-eyed. "You're a very nice fellow, too. And, if I had to lay money on it…" She thumped his chest with a pointy finger, and—*ow!*—that kind of hurt. "I'd say you're the man for Joy, not Giacomo."

Devon viewed Lou with dismay. "But, Joy's made her choice," he said hoarsely.

"Has she?" Lou questioned earnestly. "Or, did you decide for her?"

"Me?"

"Yes, you."

"But, how—"

"By being a big—please forgive the word, but it fits—*wimp*."

Now that was kind of harsh coming from normally cheerful Lou Christmas. Especially since she'd said it with that heated gleam in her eyes.

Devon raked a hand through his hair, his emotions all topsy-turvy. Of course, he loved Joy. And, naturally, he was devastated by this turn of events. Yet, those things *had* happened. Joy had already left for Florence to be with Giacomo and his family. Devon wasn't sure what Lou wanted him to say—or do.

"I'm expecting you to do the right thing," she said, stunning him by apparently reading his thoughts.

"Wait a minute. How did you—?"

"The *noble* thing," she continued undaunted. "The thing a man does when he doesn't want to make the biggest mistake of his life, and lose the woman he loves forever."

Devon swallowed hard, understanding Lou was right. This wasn't boyfriend territory anymore. This was a lifelong commitment. This was *marriage*. If Joy married Giacomo, Devon *would* lose her forever. Maybe, by virtue of his inaction, he already had. Panic reared up inside him, causing alarm bells to ring in his head. All at once, his system was on high alert, accepting the urgency of the situation. "What if it's too late?"

Lou pursed her lips and considered this a moment. Finally, she said, "Devon, can I ask you a question?"

"What's that?"

"Do you believe in fate?" She softened her tone. "Destiny?"

"I, uh…" Devon felt a rash of heat at his neck. "Think so."

"And, what do you think that means?"

"That things happen for a reason," Devon answered, his mental wheels turning, and his heart pounding harder. "And, certain things are meant to be."

"Like you and Joy?"

"I thought so. Once."

"Let me give you a little tip," Lou said gently. "Sometimes your destiny doesn't fall in your lap." She firmly patted his cheek. "You have to go out and get it."

Chapter Seventeen

JOY WAS STRIDING through the main piazza in Florence, arm in arm with Giacomo, when she heard a familiar voice call out behind her. "Joy! Joy Christmas!"

Goose bumps skittered down her spine and she stopped walking. *It can't be...* She broke away from Giacomo, spinning quickly on her heel. *But, it is!*

Devon Slade tore toward her, weaving through the thronging crowd of tourists, traversing the cobblestones, and passing by others seated at café tables lining the square.

Joy cupped her hands to her mouth in disbelief as Devon drew nearer. He was dressed in a jacket and jeans and gripped a bouquet of roses in one hand. This was so surreal on so many levels. Devon had never given Joy flowers. Ever. Not even when they were dating. And, he'd never traveled too far outside of Christmas Town. As far as Joy knew, Devon had never even been on a plane. Until, apparently, now. Joy's head spun and her heart thundered. *Devon Slade, here in Italy?*

He caught up with the couple, panting and slightly bent forward. One of Devon's hands rested on his knee, and the other held the flowers. "Joy," he said, out of breath. "I had to see you."

Giacomo shot Joy a puzzled look, and Devon addressed him. "I'm sorry, man. I really am. I'm sure you're a really great guy." Devon stood up straighter. "But, I can't let Joy do this..." Joy blinked at him and he quickly added, "Not unless she really wants to." He heaved a breath and stared at Joy. "Do you?"

Next, Devon's gaze dropped to the huge bobble of a ring she wore on her left hand and he froze. Slowly, his eyes returned to Joy's, and his face contorted in anguish. "Joy?"

"What...? Why?" Tears sprang to her eyes. "Why are you doing this now?"

"Because, I..." Devon stopped and set his chin. "I didn't want to lose you."

Giacomo set his hand on Devon's shoulder in a conciliatory fashion, and Devon bristled. "We're sorry you came all this way."

Joy stared at Giacomo and her heart broke, then she turned toward Devon and it shattered further into bits. Giacomo was such a good guy. He was there for her. He loved her. But, Devon?

Devon sent Joy a petitioning look when Giacomo released him. "I'm sorry. So, so sorry about that fight we had."

"What fight?" Giacomo asked perplexedly, but Devon persisted, ignoring him.

"And, that I didn't come after you the first time," Devon pleadingly told Joy. "Now I know that I was wrong to let you go, and I never want to make that mistake again. I've always loved you, Joy," Devon rasped hoarsely. "It's always been you."

Joy's cheeks burned hot when she suddenly understood. For her, it had always been Devon, too. Giacomo was awesome. Giacomo was impressive. Giacomo was romantic. But, Giacomo wasn't Devon.

"I'm sorry I made a mess of things before," Devon went on. "But, I'm here, now." His gray gaze washed over her, and Joy's heart skipped a beat. Then it pounded more fiercely, and started beating even harder.

"I think she's heard enough," Giacomo said with a dismissive air, before turning to Joy. "Come, *cara*." He attempted to slip his arm around Joy's shoulder, but Joy backed away.

"Giacomo," she said sadly. "I'm sorry." Then, her gaze snagged on the rosebud bouquet in Devon's grasp, and she experienced a zapping *jolt*. Every single one of the rosebuds had bloomed open. And, she'd done that. She and Devon.

Joy stared up at Devon, noting tiny white dots in the air. Remarkably, it was starting to snow. And, snow was a rare occurrence in Florence. It happened, but not very often. Certainly not like it did in Christmas Town.

Giacomo stretched out a hand, catching a few small flakes in his palm. "I can't believe it," he said, looking around in amazement. "It's snowing!"

Joy stared into Devon's eyes, headily lost in his gaze... The gaze that was calling her home. To the mountains of East Tennessee, where her heart belonged...

"Come home with me, Joy," Devon said huskily. "Come back with me to Christmas Town, where we can be together—and build a family. Just like we promised we would back then."

Without taking her eyes off Devon, Joy slowly removed Giacomo's ring. "I'm sorry," she whispered, turning to him. Joy deposited the ring in Giacomo's outstretched hand, and tears warmed her eyes. "I really am."

Devon dropped his bouquet to the ground and got down on one knee, taking Joy's hand. "Joy Christmas," he said, evidently not caring that Giacomo was watching. Nor minding that half of Florence was there, with people starting to yelp with happy glee and revel in the unusual snowflakes that were falling all around them and dusting the piazza powdery white. "You're the only girl for me." Devon stopped and corrected himself. "The only *woman* for me. The woman I want by my side for a lifetime. I'll do everything in my power to support you...and love you..." Devon's Adam's apple rose and fell. "Until we both grow really old, and even longer than that."

Joy gasped as snow coated his choppy dark hair, giving her a picture of Devon as an old man, and what a wonderful, heartwarming portrait it was.

Devon dug into his jacket pocket and extracted a ring box. "This may not be as huge and magnificent as

your other ring, but it's the best my money could buy."
He flipped open the ring box and continued his
heartfelt plea. "I'll do anything you ask. Just name it.
I'd lasso the moon and net all the stars...give you
heaven and earth—if you'd let me. Because I love you
more than anything." His gray eyes misted over. "More
than *everything*. Marry me, Joy. Please say that you'll
be mine."

Heat prickled the backs of Joy's eyes, as she
viewed the shimmering half-carat diamond solitaire
ring. "Oh, Devon." Then she cut a sidelong glance at
Giacomo. "*Oh, Giacomo*," Joy blubbered apologetically
through her tears.

Giacomo nodded in understanding and
gracefully stepped back. To her amazement, Giacomo
didn't appear angry. Instead, he grinned. And, his smile
was warm and tender. Giacomo pulled his hands apart
then he began clapping them together very slowly, in a
loud and determined fashion.

"*Bravo*," he said approvingly to Devon. "That's
true love."

People cheerily shouted more *bravo*s and things
in Italian about *il amore*, and Joy saw that a group of
spectators had formed around her and Devon, as

Giacomo graciously took his leave from them in the square.

Joy watched Giacomo walk away with a tug at her heartstrings. He was such a good man. There was bound to be the right person waiting for him somewhere. Joy believed that with her whole heart. She trusted that Giacomo knew that, too. Joy hadn't yet told Giacomo about her family secrets, because she hadn't been able to work up the nerve to confide in him. Now, she understood it wasn't only about finding the courage to tell Giacomo the truth. She hadn't been able to convince herself, beyond a doubt, that Giacomo was her destiny.

Though Joy had tentatively agreed to Giacomo's proposal, somewhere deep inside, she hadn't been able to help but believe she was making a terrible mistake. Now, standing here with Devon in the snow in Italy, Joy knew why. It was because her heart already belonged to somebody else, and it had for quite some time.

She stared down at Devon and her brow rose, as the bystanders around them began chanting, urging them on. "It appears we have an audience."

"Then, I hope you'll give me an answer," Devon said, and his grin warmed her soul.

This was what Joy had hoped for, the moment she'd dreamed of, since she was seventeen, and now it was real. "My answer is yes," she said, smiling broadly. "Yes, Devon Slade, I'll marry you."

Devon slid the ring on her finger, then she tugged him to his feet and into her arms, as the crowd went wild with whistles and cheers.

Devon pulled Joy up against him and held her close.

"Thanks for coming to Florence," she sighed.

"I would have flown to Australia for you."

"Oh yeah?"

"Yeah."

"Anything I want, huh?"

Devon rested his forehead against hers. "Anything at all."

"So, if I want to visit the Maritime Provinces, that would be cool?"

Devon chuckled warmly. "We could even take your toboggan."

Joy ran a hand down his stubbly cheek, delighting in the manly feel of him. He apparently hadn't shaved since his plane had landed. Probably because he hadn't had time, in his rush to get here. To her. His one and only. And Devon Slade was, without a doubt, the only guy for her.

"I made a Christmas gift for you, too," she said sassily.

"Oh, really?"

"You know that cute little house?"

"The one on Mistletoe Lane?" Devon guessed accurately.

"I painted it for you."

Devon's lips brushed over hers, and Joy's breath shuddered. "I can't wait to see the painting, and the house."

"It's for sale, you know."

"What fortuitous timing."

Devon kissed her sweetly, and Joy's spirit felt light. So light, she believed she could fly. But not here. Not now. *Later. And most certainly with Devon.*

"Devon?"

"Yeah?"

Joy smiled softly and whispered, "Let's go home and make some Christmas magic."

The End

A Note from the Author

THANKS FOR READING *His Christmas Joy*. I hope you enjoyed it. If you did, please leave a review at the site where you purchased this book or on Goodreads.

I'm excited to share that there is one more book in the Christmas Town series. Noelle Christmas's story is next. Information on her book follows.

Come home this Christmas to...
CHRISTMAS TOWN, TENNESSEE
Where everyday dreams come true!

**New York Times and USA Today bestselling
author Ginny Baird completes her
heartwarming holiday series...**

NOELLE'S BEST CHRISTMAS
(Christmas Town, Book 8)

Fledgling newspaper reporter Noelle Christmas is
assigned to write a story on the Christmas Cookie Shop
and the famous Virginia Cookies sold there. Handsome
photojournalist Tom Wilson is sent along to help her.
Once their investigation begins, Tom is thrown by what

appears in his camera's viewfinder, versus what gets recorded as photos. Noelle is in for a few surprises too, including romantic feelings that emerge each time that Tom is near. When the pair unearths an old, never-published article on the Christmas Cookie Shop, they're faced with certain truths that could affect their futures. Can Tom, who is falling for pretty Noelle, dare to believe in Christmas magic and open up his heart?

The second of two closing novellas wrapping up the Christmas Town series.

Previously Released:

His Christmas Joy (Christmas Town, Book 7)

Learn more about Christmas Town!

www.ginnybairdromance.com

Author Bio

NEW YORK TIMES and *USA Today* bestselling author Ginny Baird has published novels in print and online and received screenplay options from Hollywood for her family and romantic comedy scripts. Whether writing lighthearted romantic comedy or spine-tingling romantic suspense, she delights in delivering heartwarming stories. Ginny is the author of the Christmas Town series, the Holiday Brides series, the Summer Grooms series, a Romantic Ghost Stories series, and several standalone books. She invites you to visit her website and connect with her on social media. http://www.ginnybairdromance.com/

Books by Ginny Baird

New!

Christmas Town Series

The Christmas Cookie Shop

A Mommy for Christmas

Only You at Christmas

The Doctor Orders Christmas

A Glorious Christmas

A Corner Church Christmas

His Christmas Joy

Noelle's Best Christmas

Holiday Brides Series

The Christmas Catch

The Holiday Bride

Mistletoe in Maine

Beach Blanket Santa

Baby, Be Mine

Jingle Bell Babies

.

Summer Grooms Series

Must-Have Husband

My Lucky Groom

The Wedding Wish

The Getaway Groom

Romantic Ghost Stories

The Ghost Next Door (A Love Story)

The Light at the End of the Road

The House at Homecoming Cove

Romantic Comedy

Real Romance

The Sometime Bride

Santa Fe Fortune

How to Marry a Matador

Counterfeit Cowboy

The Calendar Brides

My Best Friend's Bride

The Borrowed Boyfriend

Tara (Beach Brides, Book 2)

Crazy for You

Bundles

Christmas Magic:
The Entire Holiday Brides Series
(Books 1–5)
The Holiday Brides Collection
(Books 1—4)
A Summer Grooms Selection
(Books 1—3)
Romantic Ghost Stories
(Books 1–3)
Real Romance and The Sometime Bride
(Gemini Editions 1)
Santa Fe Fortune and How to Marry a
Matador
(Gemini Editions 2)
My Best Friend's Bride and The Borrowed
Boyfriend
(Gemini Editions 3)
Wedding Bells Bundle

Short Story

Special Delivery
(A Valentine's Short Story)

Made in the USA
Columbia, SC
01 February 2021

32053685R00105